FACE

USA TODAY BESTSELLING AUTHOR
C.J. PINARD

This book is an original publication of Pinard House Publishing.

This is a work of fiction. The names, characters, places, and incidents are products of the writer's imagination or have been used fictitiously and are not to be construed as real. Any resemblance to persons, living or dead, actual events, locales, or organizations is entirely coincidental.

Copyright © 2022 Pinard House Publishing, LLC

This is licensed for your personal enjoyment only. No part of this book may be reproduced, scanned, or distributed in any printed or electronic format without permission. Please do not participate in, or encourage, piracy of copyrighted materials in violation of the author's rights. Purchase only authorized editions. All rights reserved.

PRINTED IN THE UNITED STATES OF AMERICA

ISBN: 9798800857665

ACKNOWLEDGEMENTS

Cover Art by Kellie Dennis at Book Cover by Design

Copyediting by Amabel Daniels

Proofreading: Heather Carver

Photo used with exclusive permission.

NIGHTHAWKS MC SERIES
Viper

Shadow

Phoenix

Venom

Face

"The face is the mirror of the mind, and eyes without speaking confess the secrets of the heart." ~St. Jerome

1

HACKER'S PARADISE

I twirled the pencil nervously between my fingers as the multiple lines of code stared back at me from the monitor. I was determined to figure out how these damn hackers got through to our servers. Even more concerning was that I hadn't told Viper—or anyone—about the breach. Don't get me wrong, I would eventually, but the way I saw it, if I told him now, he'd just tell me to handle it. I did, however, think it was time for me to solicit some help.

"What's up?" Jemini asked as she popped her head into my office in response to my text to meet me here.

I indicated the chair in front of my desk. "Have a seat."

She sat and frowned, presumably at the look on my face. "What's wrong?"

The thing about Jemini was... she was very intuitive. I knew she had a mother for a witch but was never a practicing one before she was turned against her will into a vampire, but I tended to think there was some kind of psychic thing going on with her—and part of me wondered if she even knew she had it. It was like women's intuition on steroids.

"We've been hacked, and I need your help," I replied.

Her eyes widened. "Oh no. When did it happen?"

I set the pencil down and folded my hands together on the desk. "About a week ago."

"Show me," she said, coming around the desk.

I had four computer monitors set up, and I pointed to the one on the right. "See this here? It's some kind of malware."

She nodded. "You're correct, it looks like spyware." She looked down at me. "The antivirus software isn't booting it out?"

"No, it only detects it," I said, shaking my head. "Look." I ran the software and showed that it failed to get rid of the bug. "It's already wormed into our comms, even after I put patches on everything and updated the firewall."

She bit her lip and shook her head. "Not good."

"I can't manually remove it, either. I tried." I raked my hand through my hair.

"Obviously, you've tried Googling it," she asked.

"Yes, but I'm not getting anything useful. Results pop up mostly for personal PCs. This isn't the most complex system, but it's way more than a simple operating system, and this bug is more than a dumb trojan horse."

She laid her hand on my shoulder. "We'll figure it out. Let me call one of my former coworkers, Mack. I'll be vague. He's got a pretty big brain."

"Thanks, Jemini," I murmured as she walked out, typing on her phone.

I looked back at the screen and blew out a breath. It wasn't like the answer was just going to pop out at me, no matter how long I stared at it. If Jemini's friend didn't have any solutions, I might have to consult the Dark Web, which I really didn't want to do. Accessing it a few days ago may have been what caused the malware to begin with. I wasn't sure. I hadn't downloaded anything suspicious, nor had I even plugged in anything external like a USB. I had backup drives always plugged in, so it couldn't have come from those. I had only accessed a human trafficking site I'd stumbled on recently. I sometimes sent anonymous tips to the local police whenever I found illegal stuff on the Dark Web. This particular site I was tracking carefully, watching when they'd move their operation location. When they eventually came to New Orleans, there would be no police involved. Nighthawks would be taking care of that, BSI be damned. Those humans weren't going to continue to get away with that shit.

"Knock, knock."

I looked up to see Kalissa standing in the doorway. "Come in, take a load off." I pointed to her large, swollen belly and then to the chair.

"Thanks," she replied, slowly taking a seat.

I stopped breathing in through my nose in hopes I could tamp down the hunger that rallied in me whenever she was around.

She held up her cell phone and said, "Can you help me with something?"

"Sure," I said, taking it from her. "What's wrong?"

"Whenever I access the browser, it just keeps closing on me. It's frustrating, especially when I'm trying to buy something and have to start over."

As I located the icon for the browser, I said, "I've been meaning to set up a small PC station in the clubhouse for people to use for whatever they need. You've motivated me to get that done this week." I tapped the icon and went to a major online shopping retailer. I put some stuff into the "cart" and sure enough, the browser shut down. "Let me make sure you don't have a virus, first."

What was it with me and computer viruses today? I ran a quick scan and found nothing. Then, I logged her out of the browser, uninstalled it, then reinstalled it. I handed the phone back to her and told her to log in and try again.

After pushing a few buttons, she looked up at me and smiled. "I think it's working now. It's faster, too. Thanks, Parker."

I smiled back at her, still breathing through my mouth. "You're welcome. Just come back if it shuts down again. Oh, and I put a bunch of stuff in your Amazon cart to test the site, so you might want to check that before you check out."

"Will do," she said before waddling out.

I sucked in a big breath I really didn't need and swallowed down the extra saliva in my mouth from when it had been watering. I had obviously learned how to control my thirst for blood while around humans, but her scent was especially strong, and her heartbeat louder than others' due to her pregnancy. I would never hurt her but being that I mostly stayed at the clubhouse around vampires all the time, human scents were stronger for me. It was the same when Bloome started hanging out here with Shadow. Thankfully she had sensed my unease and now sprayed some kind of pheromone on her that masked her human scent. I wanted to ask her to give it to Kalissa but didn't know if it was safe for pregnant women. I needed to learn to control it, anyway.

My club brothers seemed to all find wives and girlfriends within the last year. I was grateful for the expensive noise-canceling headphones I'd found online since they were all going at it every single night these days. I wasn't sure if I wanted to be bothered being in a relationship right now, anyway. I was only twenty-six in calendar years and knew I had forever to find someone, so it was low on the priority list.

A beep from the computer brought my attention back to the task at hand. The antivirus software had detected another breach. I immediately opened the notification and saw another piece of malware being threaded into our system. I quickly clicked on it and ordered the antivirus software to get rid of it. The software obeyed, but when I checked the internal systems, the virus was still there. This was the third time today. Who was trying to infiltrate our system? Jemini had been right—it was spyware. So, someone wanted to look at the inner workings of our system. I put up more patches and another firewall in hopes that would make it difficult for whoever or whatever was trying to get in.

Stretching my back, I realized I had been sitting in this chair too long. A glance at the clock on the computer told me it was almost one a.m. I'd been working on this problem since the sun went down seven hours ago, and I needed a break. After snatching my keys and phone from the desk drawer, I walked out into the clubhouse and made my way to the breakroom.

"What's up?" Venom asked as he sat at the table with Kalissa. They were both eating some kind of pasta with what smelled like seafood in it.

Trying to breathe through my mouth only, I put on a smile. "Nothing. Just needed a break. Gonna grab a drink and head to the gym." I pointed to the fridge.

I pulled a blood bag from the fridge. After dumping it into an obnoxious coffee mug that read *Eat Me* with a picture of a mouth depicting fangs dripping blood, I popped it into the microwave and waited for it to warm up. Kalissa tried to hide the revulsion on her face but failed.

"Thank you for helping her out," Venom said, pointing to his woman with his fork. "She told me you fixed her phone."

I chuckled. "Her phone was fine. Her browser was corrupted. I just re-installed it. Easy stuff."

"Easy for you," Venom said before he forked the food into his mouth.

"You got a little sauce on your shirt," Kalissa said, reaching across the table with a napkin in her hand. She wiped his black tee with it.

"Don't you have to be at work in a few hours?" I asked her.

She smiled at me. "I quit the clinic. After the baby's born, I'll see about some part-time work, if need be."

"There will be no need," Venom replied. Reaching over, he rubbed her big belly while staring at her as if she was the most important person on earth.

Give me a break.

The microwave beeping saved me from replying. I removed the cup, drank all the blood in one long gulp, and put the mug into the sink. "I'm heading to the gym," I said, not sure why I was repeating myself.

"Have a good workout," Shadow said as I damn near bumped into his tall ass while he entered the breakroom as I was walking out.

"Thanks," I murmured, heading up to my room to change into my workout gear.

The whole reason I came to the gym at this time of night/morning was to get in a workout in peace. Yes, it was a twenty-four-hour-type operation, but it was rare to see any more than like four humans here at this time of night. Tonight, there were over a dozen. One male was currently occupying my favorite treadmill, which made me instantly irritated. Why, I wasn't sure, but that damn malware attack had put me in a bad mood.

With my enhanced eyesight, I could see he had twelve minutes left on his workout. I didn't want to wait, and I couldn't very well order him off the machine, so I begrudgingly took the one next to him. His treadmill was my favorite because I'd programmed my own workout speed and set into it and all I had to do was punch a button. Annoyed, I fiddled with the buttons on my machine to start the workout and then pulled my earbuds from my pocket. They were already plugged into my phone, and after starting the techno music playlist, I began a fast jog to get me warmed up.

In truth, I didn't really need the workout. It had admittedly become part of a routine that I'd started while I was still human four years ago, and it stuck. Being a vampire seriously sucked, if I was honest with myself. I didn't like the lack of the "high" I used to get from the endorphins and adrenaline coursing through my body after a good forty-five-minute run, but I still did it, nonetheless. As vampires, we lacked fully functioning eccrine glands that caused us to sweat, so occasionally, I would have to remind myself to squirt my water on my face to maintain the façade that I was perspiring like a normal human. I watched the television set right in front of my favorite treadmill that the asshole was currently inhabiting. The pain from exercise wasn't the same as it had been when I was human. My muscles would ache, but it never lasted long. When I was human—even though I was still very young—I would be sore for days after a long run or some weightlifting. Now, it only hurt for a brief time while I'd exercise.

As the techno music blasted in my ears, I kept my eyes fixated on the TV. The sitcom playing helped distract me from checking the time every five minutes. The closed-captioning on the television helped me to get engaged in the program while the techno kept me pumped and running at a good speed. A few minutes into it, a tap on my shoulder bolted me out of the zone. Irritated, I turned to see who'd touched me, and frowned.

"What?" I asked the douche who'd taken "my" treadmill.

"Parker Knight?" he queried.

Panting, I replied, "Yes?"

"This you, dude?" He handed me my Louisiana state driver's license.

I continued to run but stared down at the ID as my feet pounded on the belt. "Yeah, it is." I panted as if out of breath. "Where did you get this?"

"It was in the cupholder of the treadmill I was just on. I got here earlier and saw it in there, put it in my pocket, and was gonna hand it into the front desk. But then I seen you look just like the photo there," he drawled, pointing to the ID.

What in the hell... why was my driver's license in the cupholder?

I shoved it into my pocket. "Well, thanks. Yes. I must have left it here."

"No problem, man." He walked away, wiping a towel over his head and face.

Continuing to run, I racked my brain, trying to figure out why my ID had been in the cupholder. Then I remembered that the last time I was here, a few days ago, I'd had to show my ID to get into the gym, as I couldn't get their glitchy app to pull up the barcode on my phone to get me into the gym. They'd had to look me up manually in the system. I'd set the license into the cupholder at the time and had obviously forgotten about it. Good thing I hadn't been pulled over driving here on my bike. I watched the guy walk away. Even though he'd taken my favorite treadmill, the guy wasn't a douche. That title belonged to me for being so careless.

I used the showers after my workout and headed to the tanning area in the back. Thankful for the 24-hour automated spray tan booth, I put my credit card in, stripped down to nothing, then stepped inside and let the jets do their thing. Being a vampire sucked enough as it was, and I wasn't ready to embrace the pale yet. One day I was sure I'd stop but for now, it gave me a sense of normalcy, a dash of humanity, and maybe a little control since nothing in my life was as it used to be. When they took notice, I'd told my club brothers this was for my mental health, and they stopped razzing me about it.

HELL'S ANGEL

I walked into the clubhouse feeling much better and less annoyed. The treadmill gave me time to brainstorm about my current problem, and I decided the first thing I had to do was come clean with Viper, the club's president.

I popped my head into his office, where he sat behind the computer, looking frustrated as usual. "Hey, boss. Got a sec?"

He peered around his monitor and waved me in. "Come on in."

I took a seat and said, "How are things going? Any computer issues?"

"No," he replied. "How was your tan?"

Chuckling, I asked, "Is it that obvious?"

He wrinkled his nose. "No, I can smell it."

"Yeah, it smells pretty gross. Thankfully, it fades in a few hours. Should have brought some cologne with me."

"What's on your mind, Face?" He folded his hands on his desk.

"I wanted to let you know about a little problem I'm having with the system. I keep encountering malware, and I believe it's coming from an outside source. I've put on countless patches, and updated the firewalls and virus software, but I can't seem to get rid of the spyware completely. And when I manage to, it worms its way back into our comms."

"In English?" Viper deadpanned.

I frequently had to remind myself how old my club brothers were. Most of them had been already very old by the time computers and most of modern technology had been invented. They didn't grow up with it like I had. Smiling, I said, "We have a computer virus that I can't get rid of. I think someone is trying to hack into our systems."

He frowned. "For what purpose?"

"That's what we're trying to figure out, but I thought it only fair that I let you know."

He shifted in his seat and leaned back. "What exactly is this spyware doing? I mean, from the name of it I assume it's spying on stuff on our system?"

I shrugged. "Sort of. I can't nail down the type of spyware it is exactly, but it does seem to be a type of bug that mostly spies on what we're doing. It hasn't really infected anything like a virus would. It's more like watching what we do rather than stealing information... I believe."

"That's not good. How long has it been happening?" he asked.

"About five days, give or take." I sighed.

He nodded. "I see. Do you need to call in some outside help? Humans good with computers? I'll pay whatever it costs."

"I will consider that next; however, Jemini has an old colleague she's going to call. She promised to be discreet."

"Very well. In the meantime, is there anything you need from me or anyone in the club?"

"Yes, can you call church soon? I need to brief everyone on what they need to be aware of with their tablets and phones."

Viper looked at his watch. "I'll call church in five."

"Thanks, boss. And look, I'm sorry I didn't tell you about it sooner."

He looked at me hard for a few long seconds then said, "I understand. Just make sure you keep me in the loop from now on, no matter how small the issue. You dig?"

I bit back a smile at the use of his favorite old-school term. "I dig."

Five minutes later, we were all in the main area of the Cobalt Room.

Viper stood at the podium. "Sorry for the short notice. Face has some things he needs to go over with you guys." He looked at me and stepped away from the podium. "Face?"

"Thanks, boss." I looked out at the prospects, lieutenants, and their old ladies. Jemini stood next to me for support. "Look, I'm going to just cut to the chase. There's been a breach in our computer system. Someone or something is attempting to inject spyware onto our systems. This isn't a virus, but something that's watching things like keystrokes and website visits. I would urge all of you to not say anything that will incriminate yourself or bring attention to the club. Do not send texts or emails about vampires or anything supernatural. Don't visit websites to look up anything to do with the supernatural. Regular websites for shopping, searches, and that type of stuff is fine. If you must text, do it in code, but it's preferable you use the phone and call the person because we're fairly sure that can't be recorded. I'm going to install a computer in the main area of the club for you to use for whatever you'd like. It's going to have bare minimum WiFi and no connection to our intranet's main system. So, if you must look up something questionable, do it on there. Or if you're just tired of online shopping on your phones and tablets." I looked at Kalissa and her blue eyes twinkled in amusement.

Jemini added, "We're sorry about this, but we'll get it taken care of soon. In the meantime, I'm sorry to ask but you're going to have to turn your location services off on the phones and tablets for now. The malware may be tracking where you're going. We don't need whoever's watching us to know our every move."

Viper asked, "Is that it?"

I looked at Jemini and she nodded. "Yes, boss." She looked at the crowd. "Just know we're on top of it."

"Questions?" Viper asked the crowd.

Andy, our newest lieutenant, raised his hand. "Do we know

who's doing it?"

"No." I shook my head. "Totally anonymous. We couldn't even track where in the country or even the world it's coming from. This person or persons are good."

"I'm here if you need anything," he replied.

"Thanks, Andy," I said.

Dash raised his hand. "You good if I get a burner phone to use in the meantime?"

I glanced at Viper. "Boss?"

"It's your call," Viper replied to me.

"That's fine, just keep your main one on so we can contact you, if need be."

Dash nodded.

"Anyone else?"

At the lack of questions, I left the podium.

"Adjourned," Viper said, pounding the gavel.

The next night, Jemini came into my office looking excited. "Got a sec?"

"Of course." I indicated the chair.

She sat and said, "How's it going? Any luck?"

"Not really. I was able to isolate one and remove it, then program the system to reject it next time it tries to worm in."

"Well, I talked to my friend. He said he can't help but he knows someone who can."

"Great," I said with a smile and some relief.

"Slight problem, though…" She hesitated.

I furrowed my brow. "What is it?"

She chewed her lip and answered, "He said she's somewhat, ah, shady—but good. Works for cash only, and… get this… will only meet at night."

I lifted my right eyebrow. "Vampire?"

She shrugged one shoulder. "Could be, but I couldn't exactly ask him that, ya know? I set up a meeting with her for tomorrow night."

"Okay… and her credentials? I mean, what makes your friend think she can help us?"

Jemini's lips twitched. "She's apparently a very skilled hacker."

I thought about this and realized we didn't have much to lose. If she was indeed a vampire, that would make things easier. I hoped. "Okay, well, we can just hope for the best, I guess."

"Gabe and I are headed out to the Devil's Den for a bite. You coming with?"

I looked at the computer screens, realizing how much work I had to do, but also remembering I hadn't eaten today. The last sustenance I'd had was that mug yesterday before the gym. I hated that I needed to feed more often than my older brothers, but Jemini understood since she was an even newer vampire than me. She and her boyfriend Phoenix, another lieutenant here, frequented the vampire bar more often than not. "Sure, let's go."

Jemini held onto Phoenix as they weaved their way through the streets of New Orleans with me trailing behind on my Harley. Once we reached the small, dark club, we parked our bikes out back and wandered inside.

The couple ordered whiskey, but I rarely drank and didn't see any reason to start now. As a vampire, the alcohol metabolized too quickly to catch any kind of buzz. In college, I'd done enough drinking to last me the rest of my existence.

"Club soda, man," I said to the bartender.

I looked around and saw all the blood whores and fellow vampires, and wondered how this place even stayed in business. They didn't serve food and the cocktails weren't very expensive. I assumed it was the humans who drank to relax before they got their life force sucked out by a preternatural creature such as myself.

It hadn't taken Phoenix and Jemini long to find themselves a donor. As the human blonde sat on Phoenix's lap with his mouth to her neck, Jemini suckled at the woman's wrist with her eyes closed. I looked away and quickly spotted a woman in the darkest corner of the bar. She had long black hair and an exotic look to her. Her lips tipped up in a smile, and when she held her drink up to me, I knew that was a cue that she was available.

"I'm Parker," I said, taking the empty chair across from her.

"Angel," she replied with a smile. "You hungry, gorgeous?"

I nodded. "Yes, babe. Come have a seat." I patted my lap. No use in pleasantries or small talk. We both only wanted one thing.

Setting her drink down, she grinned before slinking into my lap and wrapping her slender arms around my neck. Then, she leaned in and kissed me on the mouth as I ran my hand down her back and squeezed her ass. I kissed my way down to her jugular, the throbbing vein begging me to bite into it. Angel moved her sleek black hair to the side and seemed to push her neck out to me. Licking my lips, I felt my fangs descend and then quickly inserted them into her jugular. The blood flowed perfectly as I swallowed it down.

Angel moaned in my ear. "Yes. God, yes."

My dick was stiff like it always was when I fed, and as I sucked down more of her deliciously sweet blood, I tried to remember the last time I got laid. It had been weeks if not months. Another blood whore.

Concentrate, Parker!

I listened to her heartbeat, which was still fairly strong, but told myself to stop feeding. Reluctantly, I pulled my teeth from her neck and then licked the wound slowly. I felt Angel shudder in my arms.

"Holy shit, I'm so horny," she whispered in my ear. "Wanna get out of here and continue this elsewhere, gorgeous?"

Definitely couldn't say no to that. "Lead the way, babe."

As Angel dragged me by the hand, I waved at Phoenix, who was ordering another drink from the server at the table, and walked out the door of the bar with this blood whore to release some pent-up frustration. Her blow job in the alley behind the bar did not disappoint.

3
CLOAK & DAGGER

"I feel like I'm in a spy movie," Jemini said, looking around the dark alley as she crossed her arms over her black tank top. Lights from the mouth of the alley reflected off her black leather pants.

I glanced around. "You're not wrong. This is weird as hell."

She checked her phone. "It's five past midnight. Where is she?"

"Where's Phoenix?" I asked as we waited for this mysterious stranger to show up.

"He's... close by." She winked at me.

"I'm guessing he's not alone," I deadpanned.

"You would be correct."

Movement from my peripheral vision caught my eye and we both turned to see a figure standing at the mouth of the alley. They were slight in build, with dark clothing, including a hoodie over their head.

"Hello?" Jemini called out.

"Just wait," I whispered.

"Shoot," Jemini said quietly. "I just remembered. Mack said not to stare or comment on her face."

I looked at her, puzzled. "What does that mean?"

We watched as the hooded figure began to slowly walk down the alley toward us. Then, in a blink, they were right in front of us.

"Vampires," the person whispered in a voice too high to be

male.

"Correct," I replied, standing stock-still with my arms folded over my cut.

Jemini asked, "Are you the one Mack referred to us?"

She nodded, but I still couldn't see her face. "Yes. You're Face and Jemini?"

"Yes," we answered in unison.

"What's the password?" the stranger asked.

"What's with the Cloak and Dagger bullshit?" I snapped back.

"Password." She put her hands in her hoodie pockets and looked both ways down the alley.

Paranoid, much?

"Keylogger," Jemini replied.

I looked down at my partner in question, then back to the stranger.

"I'm Rocky," she said. "What's the issue you needed help with?"

Glancing around, I said, "Malware. Are we doing this here?"

Rocky lifted a shoulder and let it fall. "We need WiFi. So, you'll have to bring me back to your office or wherever you have your computers so I can check out the problem."

I pulled the laptop I'd brought out of the bag and opened it up. "I'm not comfortable with that, so I guess we do it here, unless you'd like to go to a café or something. I have an external hotspot I can use for service."

I was frustrated that I couldn't see this person's face. Her hood was still up, and I could see eyes the color of fresh grass staring up at me, but nothing else. It made her seem untrustworthy and sketchy. Though—hadn't Jemini warned me she wasn't exactly on the up and up?

"I don't do bright places," Rocky replied. "But if you want to meet at Zombies, they have good WiFi there."

"That's fine," I said. "Meet you there."

Rocky blitzed down the alley in the blink of an eye, and once she was out of sight, I told Jemini I'd meet her there, knowing Phoenix would give her a ride.

The owner of Zombies, Theo, shook my hand and provided us with a private back room to conduct our business. He seemed to be familiar with Rocky.

"Thanks, Theo. I owe ya one."

He grinned at me before straightening his tie. "Next time my computers take a shit, I'll be calling in that favor."

I chuckled. "Absolutely."

Briefly nodding to Phoenix and Venom, who sat in a corner sipping on drinks, I made my way to the back room with Jemini and Rocky following me. After closing the door, I pulled the laptop from the messenger bag and set it on the table. Rocky and Jemini stood, waiting for the system to boot.

Typing in commands, I brought up the lines of code that showed the malware.

"That's spyware," Rocky said.

"No shit, Sherlock," Jemini replied, rolling her eyes. Then she folded her arms across her chest. "Mind losing the hood? We're indoors."

Slowly, Rocky lowered the hood from her head, and I bit back a gasp. There were lines of old white scars crisscrossed on her cheeks and down her neck. Waves of light-brown hair secured in a low ponytail cascaded down her back and her brilliant green eyes held mine in an expression I could only describe as something between curiosity and unease.

Jemini replied, "Thank you."

Rocky's eyes held mine for a few more seconds before she put her gaze back on the laptop screen and pointed. "That's spyware. You need to remove it manually."

"I've tried," I replied, ignoring the fact that her eyes and voice were stirring something inside me. "It just comes back."

"Let me see," Rocky said, shooing me out of the way.

I let her access the device and watched as her long, pale fingers lithely danced across the keyboard, putting in codes to extract the malware. I'd tried some things, but this woman had much more extensive knowledge than I did. I suddenly felt like a rookie watching her. I glanced at Jemini, whose eyes were wide in awe.

"There you go, it's gone. I put a code in to make sure it can't get back in." Rocky moved out of the way.

I sat down and ran a few programs to see if the malware was indeed gone, and to my surprise, it was. I looked up at the new stranger. "Wow, you're good. I'll give you that."

"Thanks," Rocky replied, holding my gaze briefly and then looking away.

"How long have you been a vampire?" I asked her boldly, wondering if her scars were acquired before or after her transformation, but then I remembered she would have healed scarless if they came after.

She pierced me with her leafy stare and said, "Too long."

I was caught off guard when I felt the air crackle between us, and it made me uncomfortable. It wasn't like it was with a blood whore; this was something deeper. It unnerved me so I decided to dismiss it.

"I see. What do we owe you?" I asked.

"Five hundred," she replied.

Fishing five one-hundred-dollar bills from my pocket, I held them out to her silently.

Rocky took the bills, and when her soft hand brushed mine, I felt a tingle race up my arm. *What the hell is that?*

"Pleasure doing business with you," she replied, pulling the hood back over her head and disappearing out of the door.

I looked at Jemini, whose eyebrow was raised in question.

"What?" I asked.

"She was quite… uh…"

"Unique," I finished for her.

She nodded. "I agree."

"I'm gonna head back to the club. Phoenix got you?" I asked.

She nodded. "Yep."

After thanking Theo, we headed out of Zombies. I slung the messenger bag over my shoulder and hopped on my bike. The ride wasn't more than ten minutes, and once I got back to the clubhouse, I quickly made my way to my office and checked the system again. Sure enough, Rocky had removed the worst of the malware. I had carefully watched the codes she'd put in to do it and hoped it would work for any other spyware that was sure to come.

I sat back and wondered how she knew how to remove it so quickly. According to Jemini, she hadn't been told much about the type of invasion we'd been dealing with. That was why I'd asked her how long she'd been a vampire. Maybe she'd had years—even decades—to hone the craft of hacking and computer sciences. Unlike me.

After another quick scan, I texted one of the prospects, Fox, to meet me in my office. Then, I got up and went to the supply closet where I kept all my spare computer parts and extras. After selecting a CPU, two twenty-one-inch monitors, a keyboard, and a mouse, I set them on the desk just as Fox poked his head in the door.

"You rang?" he asked in his best Lurch voice.

I chuckled. "Yes. Can you help me carry these things out to the clubhouse? I'm gonna set up a station right outside the breakroom for people to use."

"Sure," he said, grabbing both monitors and the keyboard. "Great idea."

I took the rest and followed him out. I realized I needed a table and chair until I could order a real desk, so we set the stuff down on the breakroom table. I went into a supply closet and pulled out the spare table. It was small and would have to do.

Fox helped me set everything up and once I booted up the machine, I installed a local WiFi connection that was just for this particular computer in case hackers wanted to keep trying to get into our systems. Once I was satisfied with the setup, I thanked Fox before he headed back to the Cobalt Room where he was a bartender.

Viper walked up to the new setup and said, "Great idea."

"Thanks. This has a local internet connection only, so in case we're hacked again, they won't be able to access this one—I hope. It's not tied into our systems at all."

"Very nice. What's the latest on that, anyway?"

I quickly filled him in on the situation from earlier and let him know there was no more spyware or malware on the system—for now.

"That's great. Do you think we can trust this Rocky person?"

I lifted a shoulder. "Not sure. I paid her cash and didn't get her contact info. But she did get rid of the problem."

"Seems like she could be a good backup in case you run into any more problems you or Jemini can't solve," he said, piercing me with his intense hazel eyes.

"I agree. If we need her again, I'll have Jemini get in touch with her."

"Sounds like a plan." MyAnna, his wife, came up and put her arms around his waist. "Wanna come have a drink with us? Slow night all the way around," he asked.

Viper knew I rarely drank so I figured he just meant to socialize while I sipped club soda or water. "Is there something you wanted to discuss with me?"

He shook his head. "No, was just going to hang out and watch the band. If you're busy, I get it."

"I just have a few more things to do so when I'm done, I'll meet you there." I started to walk away and remembered something. "Hey, am I good to order a computer desk and chair for that station?" I pointed to it.

"Of course. Just email me the receipt so I can put it into the books."

"You got it," I replied, heading to my office.

4

HOW TO WIN FRIENDS AND INFLUENCE MONSTERS

I lifted my head when I heard shouts coming from the main part of the clubhouse. I jogged down the hall and out to the open space where I saw Jemini, MyAnna, and Bloome having a heated argument.

"Why should I be the one to do it all? You guys need to pitch in!" MyAnna said, pointing at the other two.

"I have a job here. I help Face with IT stuff and I'm busy!" Jemini replied.

Bloome folded her arms across her chest. "I don't even live here fulltime. I have my own house."

"Whoa, whoa, what's the problem, ladies?" Shadow asked as he approached them, Phoenix and Venom on his tail.

"Yeah, you're going to wake Kalissa. She has to be up in a few hours," Venom said.

"Someone has to keep this place clean. I don't mind cleaning up some, but why am I doing it all?" MyAnna cried. She was so small that I had to bite back a grin at how she just looked like an angry kitten instead of a ferocious female on a verbal rampage.

"Hey, let's take this down a notch. Everyone should be keeping their own areas clean, and not expecting anyone else to pick up after them," Viper said.

MyAnna huffed. "It's not the individual areas I'm talking about. The breakroom, for instance, I do the dishes almost every day. No, there's not many, but why can't people put their cups and dishes into the dishwasher? Wipe off the table? Sweep or mop the floor? Go to the store and stock the freezer with human food? While we're at it, the main clubhouse out here—who do you think cleans it? Sweeps up the dog hair?" She gave Venom a pointed look.

Do female vampires get PMS? I wondered.

Phoenix raised an eyebrow. "Aren't the prospects supposed to be doing that stuff?"

Viper nodded. "Yes, they are. We can't very well hire a personal cleaning company to work in here, so yes, the prospects are supposed to be keeping this place kept up."

"Just leave a broom out, I'll sweep up my own fucking fur from now on, geez," Venom said, his hands up in surrender. "And I'll go to the store, tomorrow. I'm tired of Hot Pockets, anyway."

Such a petty thing to be arguing about, I thought. If MyAnna just stopped doing it, Viper would notice and get on the prospects' asses. A few of them had fulltime jobs restoring the bikes and sometimes a car or two, but the others just tended bar or waited tables at Cobalt or watched the club. No reason they couldn't pitch in. I sometimes wondered if MyAnna was just bored and kept busy cleaning. She needed some kind of a job around here. The only thing she was responsible for was keeping an eye on Cobalt when Viper was out. I would rack my brain and try to think of something and then suggest it to Vane later.

A text took my attention away from the drama and I walked away as I pulled the phone from my pocket. It was the anonymous text line with a message: *Two underage girls kidnapped by vampires and put on a boat down on the river. Better hurry.*

Attached was a photo of three men in dark clothing escorting two young girls who couldn't be older than fifteen onto a small speedboat.

"Shit," I said, turning back around. "Boss, we got a situation." I handed him the phone.

The others crowded around and read the message.

Viper enlarged the photo and asked, "Do we know these cats?"

Nobody answered.

"Do we know where exactly that is?" Shadow asked, pointing at the screen.

Phoenix said, "Let me see that."

Viper handed him the phone.

He stared at it. "Looks like the docks where I used to work, but further down past the barges and cargo ships."

"Let's go," Viper said.

"They're probably long gone by now," Andy commented.

Viper fished his keys from his pocket. "Doesn't matter, let's ride. Lieutenants only." He turned to MyAnna and kissed her on the forehead. "Watch the club, Shortstop?"

She nodded and we headed out back to our bikes.

We parked in the lot the dock workers used for their vehicles and turned the bikes off. I looked around and didn't see anything familiar, so I pulled the phone out and looked at the photo again.

"Head south along the river, I think it's this way," Phoenix said, and we followed.

Once past the large ships, we came to a small section of shore that was unoccupied. There were footprints in the claylike sand that disappeared once they reached a dent where a boat had been docked.

"Shoe size is small, like a woman's or teen's," Andy said, bending down and tracing his finger over them. "There are larger, men-sized ones here too," he continued.

"Seems to be consistent with the photo," I said. "I wonder

where they took the picture from?" I turned around and scanned the area.

Phoenix and Shadow backtracked a little until they were in a spot where the photo was most likely taken from. "There's nothing here. Whoever took those had some balls to take pictures out in the open like this."

"Strange," Viper said. "What was the purpose of sending that text if there's nothing we can do? A description of the people and boat would have been helpful. We're chasing our tails here."

"I'm going to run the kids' faces through my software to see if I can get an ID. The faces of the men are too dark," I said.

"How did the sender know they're vampires, I wonder?" Phoenix asked.

"That was my first thought, too," I replied. "Maybe the sender followed them for a while or something? Probably a vamp himself."

"Can you reply to the text?" Andy asked.

I shook my head. "No, it's an anonymous tip line for a reason. It only allows for incoming texts."

"With no way to trace it?" he asked, incredulous.

"Nope. I've tried before," I replied.

Viper made a face. "I hate to say this but maybe we should call the BSI. They could get the FBI involved discreetly."

"But if they're vampires…" Venom said.

"I know, that's why I'd leave it up to their discretion," Viper said.

I stared down at the photo again, then back to the guys. "Don't call them just yet. Let me try a few things on our end first. If I can ID the victims, it'll give us a place to start and we can go from there."

"Okay. In the meantime, since there are no witnesses here to interview, we should go," Viper said.

"Wait," Phoenix said, putting his hand up and looking down the shore. "There are vampires on the nightshift on the docks. The humans would not have seen or heard anything, but the vamps might have."

Venom patted his friend on the shoulder. "Good call. I should have thought of that."

"Do you know any of them?" Viper asked.

Phoenix tapped his fingers on his thigh. "I doubt it. It's been fifteen years. The ones I knew would have had to move on by now."

"Worth a shot," I said with a shrug.

We headed back to our bikes, and it was decided that only Phoenix and I would go try to find a couple vampire dock workers. A group of big-ass bikers walking down to the docks would attract attention. We took off our cuts and left then on the bikes.

"I don't recognize anyone," Phoenix said as we walked toward the docks.

"Can I help you?" a man asked, seeming to come out of nowhere.

We stopped walking and I concentrated on staring at the guy, trying to determine if he was human or something else. It took me longer to recognize fellow vampires because I hadn't mastered the skill yet. Werewolves in human form were easier to identify, as they had a distinct smell.

"Yes. We're looking for Tom," Phoenix said, and I could tell he had the guy's eyes locked. Human.

The man lazily looked away from Phoenix and pointed down toward the docks.

"Thank you," Phoenix said. "You won't remember us being here. Go back into the office."

"I won't remember," he repeated robotically.

After he walked off, I asked, "Who's Tom?"

Phoenix lifted his shoulder and let it fall. "Hell if I know, just took a chance there's a Tom working here."

I chuckled. "Very stealthy of you."

A group of men were lifting crates and loading them onto large barges. I tried to see if any were vampires, but it was too difficult with them moving around so much.

"Those two," Phoenix said, pointing to a pair of guys hoisting barrels onto the ship.

"How can you tell from here?" I asked, feeling like such a rookie.

Phoenix snorted. "No human can lift three-hundred-pound barrels that easily."

"Oh," I said. "How do you know they weigh that much?"

"Because I used to work here, remember? Those are for whiskey and gin, and they're full, probably heading to Europe."

"Good to know."

Gabe grabbed my arm. "Follow me."

We approached the workers. "Excuse me, can we talk to you for a second?" Phoenix asked.

About ten men stopped what they were doing and looked at us.

"Just you two," Phoenix said to the vampires, giving them a knowing look.

"Boss, a quick break?" one asked. He was a big guy with a handlebar mustache and wore a sweater cap over his black hair. The other was shorter and stockier with large hands and a shaved head.

"Go ahead," the 'boss' replied.

We led them toward the street where nobody could hear us.

"What's up?" the bald one asked.

Now that they were standing close and I could see their mannerisms, I could tell they were vampires.

"I'm Gabe, this is Parker," he introduced us. "We're private investigators. We got a tip that two underage girls were kidnapped earlier tonight and taken out on a boat. Happened about fifty yards down the shore." Phoenix pointed down the beach. "Did you see or hear anything?"

"Vampire PIs. Now I've seen it all," the guy with the cap said. "I'm Rick, this is Tom."

I chuckled a little.

"What's so funny?" Rick asked.

"Vampire PIs, guess that's funny," I lied, not admitting that I was immaturely laughing that his name really was Tom.

"Hey, don't I know you?" Tom asked. "You look familiar."

I faked a charming smile. "Nah, I just have one of those... faces." I cringed internally. I hated that question. I got it all the damn time.

"Well?" Phoenix asked, giving me a look before putting his attention back on the duo.

"Do you know what time it happened?" Rick asked.

I looked at the timestamp on the text. "We got the tip at 2:48 a.m., so sometime around then, I assume."

The guys looked at each other. "I don't think I heard anything out of the ordinary, but these docks are so damn loud, it's hard to hear anything past it, even with our hearing," Tom said.

"No screams? No sounds of a speedboat?" I asked.

Tom snapped his fingers. "Now that you say that, yes. A couple hours ago, I saw one speed off down the river while I was on my break. I thought it was odd, this time of night."

"I saw it too," Rick added.

"Great," Phoenix replied excitedly. "Can you describe the people in the boat?"

"Well, I couldn't see them too good, but it looked like five or so people maybe?" Tom said.

"Three males, two females. The females were both blonde and looked young, the men were older, but not old. One guy wore a Pittsburgh Pirates ball cap. The boat was white with a thick red stripe down both sides. It had temporary tags taped to the front window. Oh, and the girls had something shiny on their faces," Rick finished. "Now that you say kidnapping, I'm thinking it was probably duct tape."

I lifted an eyebrow. "You saw all of that while they were speeding away?"

Rick glanced nervously at his friend then back to me. "Yeah, since I got turned, I have an insanely photographic memory. And before you tell me you think that's cool, it's not. It's only useful in times like these. The rest of the time, it's not. There are some things I wish I could just unsee, ya know?"

"I can understand that," Phoenix replied. "Were the men vampires, that you could tell?"

"No, couldn't tell, they were too far away. I could barely make out that they were men."

Phoenix put his hands in his pockets. "Anything else?"

Rick snapped his fingers. "Oh, the boat's named *The Trickster*. Other than that, nothing else."

Since he hadn't told us anything we didn't already know from the photograph, aside from confirming the boat stripe was red since the picture was dark, the name of the boat was very helpful.

"Any strange people hanging around here tonight?" Phoenix asked.

"Someone took this photo and sent it to us," I said, handing them the phone. "Recognize them?"

They looked at the picture then Rick handed the phone back to me. "No, not really. And no, I didn't see any people hanging around here who don't work here."

"Me either," Tom added.

I pulled out a business card with the anonymous tip line printed on it and nothing else. I handed it to Rick. "If you think of anything else, text it to that. It's completely anonymous, and we can't reply, but you can leave your info on there if you'd rather us call or meet with you."

He put the card in his pocket. "I will.

Once we reached the parking lot, we briefed the rest of them on what we'd been told.

"Description of the boat is about all we got to go on," Viper said.

"I'm on it. Should be easy to locate unless they changed or added the name after it was sold," I commented.

Just then, our phones all chimed in unison with a high-pitched squeal. We all looked at the screens to see a message pop up: *Child Abduction (AMBER Alert) 13 yr old Lila Green W/F/502/125 BLU/BLND and 14 yr old Terra Johnson W/F/505/145 BRO/BLND*

There was a link, so I clicked it to see photos of the girls and their last known whereabouts.

"Well, at least we have their names," I said. "What do you want to do?"

Viper's brow furrowed. "I really don't want to do this, but since it's public, we're gonna need to hand this over to the BSI and let them handle it. They'll have to figure out what to do with the men, if they are in fact vampires, once they're captured. I'm sure they've handed gray areas like this before."

"I agree," Shadow said. "Time is of the essence here. We gotta report what Rick told us and the photo."

"I'm on it," I said. "I need my computer. Meet you guys back there." I pocketed the phone, hopped on my Harley, and sped back to the clubhouse.

5

ANONYMOUS TIPSTER

"Come in," Viper said, leading the two agents into the clubhouse. It was well past five a.m. now, and I was sure we'd woken the agents, but they looked put together as usual.

He led them to the breakroom, and Viper, Phoenix, and I sat with them at the table.

"This AMBER alert, do you know anything about it?" I asked, showing them the notification on my phone.

"We've been briefed, yes," Agent Bishop replied.

I pulled up the text and showed him the photo. "We received that a couple of hours ago."

Agent Shields took the phone from me and enlarged the photo. "We received the same photo. That's why the local police issued the alert instead of waiting the customary twenty-four hours for missing persons cases."

"Makes sense," I said and then read them what the tipster had said.

"This texter say anything else?" Bishop asked, scribbling in his notepad.

"No. But know, this text line is completely anonymous. We can't reply to or trace the texts that come in," Viper added, pointing to my phone.

"I bet if you offered up a reward for any witnesses, someone might come forward," Phoenix said.

"I mentioned that to the boss after we got the photo," Agent Shields replied.

"We did talk to a couple of dock workers, one said he saw the boat. He didn't give us any information that wasn't in the photo except he confirmed the stripe is red, and also said the boat's name is *The Trickster*."

Bishop raised an eyebrow. "Oh really? You got a name for this witness?"

Phoenix looked at me questioningly. "Not sure I should say. He's a vamp who claimed to have a photographic memory. We gave him the text line in case he remembers anything else."

Bishop jotted notes into his notepad. "Forward us anything he sends you."

I nodded in acknowledgment. "Who are those girls, anyway?" I asked, just because I was curious. "I mean, we know their names, but how were they taken? The AMBER alert didn't say."

"Their parents say one was at a sleepover with the other, but there were no signs of forced entry, so they assumed the girls must have snuck out sometime during the night. No idea who took them or where they were last seen, though."

"So, whoever took that photo knows about not only us, but the BSI as well," Phoenix pointed out. "And he or she somehow knows or assumes the kidnappers are vamps."

"We need to find this person," Shields said, seeming frustrated.

"Your computer guys get a trace or anything on the sender?" I asked.

Bishop shook his head. "No, it was sent to the FBI's Crimestoppers anonymous text line, but from a burner phone which is no longer active."

I chuckled. "So, it's not actually anonymous then if they can trace it."

"No, but the reason it's called that is because they're not required to give their name, but if people want to assume the messages aren't traced, that's on them." Bishop shrugged.

"Well, it seems you guys are on top of it, so we'll back off for now," Viper said. "I hope you find the girls."

"There are rumors of human traffickers coming to the city, so we suspect this may be the start to it, unfortunately." Shields sighed.

I knew that but didn't say anything. However, I was under the impression that the traffickers were humans. I never thought they'd be vamps.

"That's terrible," Bloome said, coming into the breakroom with Shadow trailing behind her. Though, I knew she'd been eavesdropping outside the room since I could smell her pheromone perfume the whole time. "I'm happy to help with a locator spell if you bring me something personal of theirs. But I'll need an item from both girls, not just one."

"We'll take that under advisement," Shields said, looking skeptically at the witch.

"You'd be a fool to turn it down," Shadow said from behind her.

The agents stood. "Understandable. Obviously, contact us if you find out anything else," Bishop said.

Shadow and Phoenix walked the agents out.

I looked at Viper. "Still want me to see what I can dig up?"

He stood. "Of course."

"On it," I replied, getting up to head to my apartment. "But after I get some shut-eye."

My eyes widened as I hopped off the bus and looked around. The streets of Los Angeles were bustling with beautiful people, and the sun behind tall buildings cast shadows over the sidewalks.

Homeless begged for money, and street buskers played instruments in hopes of getting tips thrown into their coffee cans and upside-down hats. Adjusting my backpack on my shoulder, I looked again at the address on my phone and put on the walking directions. Seemed I had six blocks to go to reach the pay-by-the-week motel where I'd made a reservation.

"Hey, good lookin'," an older woman said as I passed. She had huge tits spilling out of her tight purple top, and her red lipstick was smeared a little. She looked drunk, or high, or both. "Need a date, sweetie?" she slurred with a lazy smile.

"No thanks," I mumbled before picking up the pace and walking faster.

I couldn't believe how crowded this place was. I had done a near-obsessive amount of research on this city, pulling up every Google Maps photo I could find to see what I was getting myself into.

Finally reaching the motel, I stopped in front of it and frowned. "This dump is ninety bucks a night?" I asked myself. With a sigh, I wandered inside and checked in. I paid for two weeks in advance before taking the card key from the clerk and heading toward my room.

I breathed a sigh of relief to see it was clean. One double bed, a dresser, and a small but functional bathroom. After unpacking my oversized backpack, I shoved it into the closet underneath the dress shirts I'd hung up. The jeans and pants I folded nicely on the rack above the shirts, and everything else went into the dresser drawers. The toiletries I stacked neatly on the bathroom counter.

Time on my phone told me I had an hour to get to the audition I had scheduled. "Shit."

I took a quick shower and put on a dress shirt and jeans, hoping the wrinkles weren't too noticeable. I pulled up a car service on my phone and ordered a ride to my destination while I perfected my hair. The phone alerted me my ride was here as I sprayed on some cologne. After snatching the folder containing my portfolio of photos, I raced out the door to my appointment.

The clock showed I had five minutes to be there, but the map app showed I still had almost three miles to go. The traffic was moving at a snail's pace, and I began to panic. I knew I wouldn't be there in time. Should I call and say I'm gonna be late?

"Ma'am. Excuse me, but is there an alternate route or something you can take?" I asked the driver.

She pulled the gum out of her mouth and set it on a cup in the cupholder before looking at me in the rearview mirror. "Nope, sorry, cutie. This is the fastest route. LA traffic is a bitch."

I never ran into traffic problems like this in Texas. Lesson learned.

I arrived six minutes late, racing into the lobby and giving the receptionist my name.

"Sorry I'm late, traffic."

"Shocking," she muttered before handing me a piece of paper with the number thirteen printed on it. "Have a seat."

"Thanks," I said, finding an empty chair in a waiting room full of men. Men... who all looked just like me.

Well, crap.

I blinked my eyes open and scrubbed a hand down my face with a groan. Why was I dreaming about events from five years ago? These dreams had been coming to me a lot lately, and I didn't like it. I picked up my phone from the nightstand and saw it was close to four p.m. I slogged out of bed and headed toward the shower.

After I was cleaned up, I took the stairs down into the clubhouse and saw Venom in his wolf form. He sat on his haunches on the concrete floor, looking at the television we had mounted near his cage. I went over and patted him on the head.

"Last night of the full moon at least, huh? You excited about being a papa soon?" I asked him.

He stared up at me and woofed softly. I didn't need him to use his yes/no squares to answer the question, I knew he was, it was all he talked about. They had decided to let the sex of the baby be a surprise, so nobody knew what to get the kid. The hens of the house were especially annoyed by this. It made me laugh.

I headed toward my office, a little sad that I'd never be a dad. I wasn't sure if I ever wanted kids, but it definitely wasn't happening now. I thought about my family back in Texas, my mom, dad, and sister. I could still see and talk to them, but Viper had told me I would have to fake my own death or something in about ten years. With a sigh, I sat down and booted up the machine until all the monitors flickered to life. After putting in my password, I frowned when the antivirus software alerted me to a problem.

"Dammit, what now?"

I clicked on the notification and saw another piece of malware had come through. I was getting sick of this crap. I isolated the malware and used what I'd seen Rocky do to remove it for good. After a few checks, I saw the computer was clean, but realized I had to do something. Thoughts of completely tearing down the system and rebuilding it from scratch filtered through my mind. But the idea of having to do that made me want to stab myself in the eye instead, since it had taken me months to build it when I first got here. Hours and hours of sleepless days. However, it was a real possibility if I couldn't stop this shit.

"What's up, buttercup?"

I looked up to see Jemini standing in my doorway holding a coffee mug that read *Have you tried turning it off and turning it back on again?*

How many damn smartass coffee mugs did we have in this joint?

"More malware," I murmured. "Got rid of it."

Her eyes widened over the rim of her bloody beverage. "Are you serious? What the hell. How does this trash keep getting in?"

I shook my head. "I wish I knew, but I'm this close to cloning the drives and then wiping it all clean. Start over with a new server."

"That sounds like a lot of work," she commented.

"It is, and if you help me, it means a lot of sleepless days to get it back up and running. I'm not ready to do that yet, though."

She sat in the chair. "Hey, didn't Rocky say she put something on the system so the malware couldn't get back in?"

"I thought so," I muttered, annoyed. "Obviously didn't work."

Jemini asked, "What can I do?"

"Well, let's teach you how to hack into NOPD's computer system. See what they got on the kidnapping of those girls."

She turned her head to the side. "I thought BSI was handling that."

"They are," I said. "But Viper told me to keep on top of it. No harm in being in step, or hell, even one step ahead of the cops."

Her green eyes sparkled with mischief as she set the mug down and pulled up a chair next to me. "Let's do it."

THERE'S SOMETHING ABOUT ROCKY

I huffed at the computer screen. "That's it, I'm scrapping the whole system."

"No, don't," Jemini said. "Let's see if that Rocky girl can help us again."

We stared at the spyware that had wormed its way in again. I was about to snap. "I'm gonna find whoever's doing this and fold their teeth back with my fist."

Jemini laid a restraining hand on my arm. "Just let's get this taken care of then you can go on your mission of violence." She pulled out her phone and hit a button. "Hi, it's Jemini from the Nighthawks." Pause. "How are you, Rocky?" Pause. "Good, thanks. We need some more help. Can you come to our clubhouse and give us a hand?" Pause. "Yeah, more malware." Pause. "Sounds good, thanks." She ended the call and then tapped the screen some more.

"She'll be here in ten minutes. I just texted her the address."

"Let me make sure Viper's cool with a stranger coming here," I said, getting up and heading toward the clubhouse.

"Boss, a word?" I said when I saw him standing at the door that led to the garage. He was talking to a prospect.

"You got it, boss," Paz said, then disappeared into the garage with a red oil rag in his hand.

"What's up?" Viper asked.

I sighed. I hated feeling like such a failure, but this problem was bigger than my ego at this point. "I can't get rid of the malware. It keeps coming back. Jemini's called in that hacker who helped us. You cool if she meets us here?"

He looked at me for a few long seconds. "Yes, but we're gonna shake her down before she comes inside."

"Cool. She'll be here in ten." I walked off before I'd have to ask for forgiveness since I hadn't asked for permission ahead of time.

A few minutes later, the doorbell buzzed throughout the space, and Jemini, Viper, Phoenix, and I headed to the door. I opened it, and those haunted green eyes were the first thing that greeted me beneath the darkness of her hood. "Come in," I said.

"Rocky, this is Viper and Phoenix. You know Jemini."

She nodded shyly. "Hi." I saw her eye the wolf with immediate fear.

"That's Venom. He won't bite. In fact, he'll be human here in a few hours."

"O…kay," she said.

"Nice to meet you. Now please lower the hood and put your arms out in a T," Viper said.

Her eyes went wide. "Why?"

"Just a little security," I tried to reassure her. I didn't like the odd, protective feeling swirling inside me.

"Oh, okay. I don't have anything on me but my phone, keys, and wallet," she replied, looking at me as she lowered her hood.

"Then this will go quickly," Phoenix said as Rocky obeyed, standing straight and putting both arms out. "Take the items out of your pocket and hold onto them."

The look on her face amped up that feeling inside me. It made me watch Phoenix a little too closely as he frisked her to make sure she had no weapons on her. I didn't like the way he patted around her hips and stomach and ran his hands down her legs and around her ankles. Her jeans were very tight, so obviously she had nothing inside them.

"She's good," he replied, stepping back.

"I told you," she murmured.

Viper nodded. "Yeah, we figured. Just a precaution."

"I would never be stupid enough to come into a houseful of big, huge vamps and try anything," Rocky said quietly.

"Come on, the office is this way," I said, just wanting her away from them and nearer to me. When I heard Viper and Phoenix start to whisper about her face as we walked off, I cleared my throat and spoke loudly. "So, no trouble finding the place?"

She shook her head as I opened my office door. "Not at all."

I ushered the girls inside. Rocky went to grab her hood and put it back over her head. In a move bold even for me, I grabbed her wrist and said, "Please don't."

Her eyes widened and she looked at my hand on her wrist, which I quickly removed. She slowly let go of the hood and let it drop to her back.

"You don't need to hide here. I don't know why you wear that hood, anyway. It hides your pretty eyes and hair." I smiled reassuringly at her.

"And my face," she murmured as a blush crept across her scarred cheeks.

"You don't need to hide that either," I said.

"Yeah, you're very pretty," Jemini said with a smile. "Beautiful bone structure."

Rocky's eyes widened again. From the look on her face, nobody had ever paid her a compliment—not recently, anyway. Made me a little sick to my stomach. If she didn't have the lines of scarring on her cheeks and neck, she could probably model. Of course, I understood why she was self-conscious, but I didn't want her hiding under that hood while she was here. I wanted her to feel comfortable in our presence.

"Thanks," she replied quietly. "Now show me what's wrong." She pointed at the computer.

The ladies pulled up chairs on either side of me while I showed them the viruses.

"That's more spyware. Did you try the extraction codes I used before?" She stared me in the eye.

I nodded. "Yes, they didn't work." God, her scent was distracting me. It was something floral like roses but also citrusy as well. It was intoxicating. "Multiple patches and firewall updates aren't working, either."

"You mind if I try something?" she asked.

"Of course not, that's why we called you." I got up and we traded seats.

She opened up a program and typed code quickly on the screen. I watched in fascination at how quickly her fingers moved and wondered what must be going on in that brilliant mind of hers. It was hard to pay attention to what she was doing because I just wanted to stare at her. I hoped Jemini was paying attention.

"Have you been on the Dark Web recently?" Rocky asked as she typed.

"Yes, I like to monitor criminal activity there."

She stopped her keystrokes and looked at me. "For what purpose?"

Before she could answer, we heard a lot of noise coming from the main area of the clubhouse. It didn't sound like an emergency, but something was definitely going on.

"Go see what's happening, please?" I asked Jemini.

"On it," she replied, getting up and rushing out of the office.

Alone at last.

"Do you know what we do here? What the Nighthawks do?" I asked her.

She smirked a little and it was so damn cute. "I'll admit to doing a little Googling."

I groaned. "I try to scrub everything about us from Google. How did you—"

She smirked wider.

"Never mind, forgot who I was talking to. And hey if you can access it, maybe next time you can scrub it for us?"

She lifted a shoulder and let it fall. "Eh, I'll think about it."

We stared at each other for a long time. Finally, she asked, "How did a pretty boy like you get involved in a biker gang? You look like you should be wearing a suit and working in a high rise, closing deals."

"First off, it's a club, not a gang. Secondly, looks can be deceiving. I obviously am not the muscle around here, but I help out when I can when we go on missions."

Her full pink lips twitched. "Missions?"

I nodded, staring at her mouth a little too long. Our faces were less than a foot apart, and the air between us was sizzling with something I'd never felt with anyone. I could tell she felt it, too. I had the overwhelming desire to kiss her, and as I began to lean toward her as if I had no control over my body, the door flung open and Rocky gasped with a jerk.

"Kalissa's water broke!" Jemini said excitedly.

I frowned. "But Venom's the wolf."

"Bloome and Shadow are driving her there in her car, and Venom's gonna have to pray she doesn't have that kid until morning."

I shook my head. "Poor Harlan."

"Wait," Rocky said. "Who's Harlan?"

"He's the wolf. Venom," Jemini supplied.

"He has a pregnant wife, or girlfriend, or whatever? Is she a wolf, too?" Rocky asked, and I was smiling inside that she was starting to feel more comfortable here.

"She's human," Jemini said, taking a seat next to us.

"So... her baby is gonna be half human, half werewolf?" She made a face.

I chuckled. "No, wolves breed with humans all the time. The babies are full werewolf; however, they don't turn into one until around age eighteen." My lips twisted in amusement at her expression. "Guess you never Googled that, huh?"

She shrugged and shook her head. "No, I don't like wolves, they scare me. Not that I've ever met one. Just what I was told. I don't see many here."

"They're pretty scarce here. Harlan's from Colorado. Big population there." I winked.

"Remind me to stay away from Colorado, then," Rocky replied with a headshake. "Now, let's finish this."

Jemini and I watched as she continued to type and then ran a scan to show the malware was gone.

"That's great, but the problem is, it keeps coming back," I said.

"I know, I'm gonna check something next." Then, she opened up the Dark Web and looked at my browsing history. I was glad I hadn't looked at anything like porn because if you wanted the hardcore stuff, that was where you went. She pointed to the page I frequented. "See that site? It's full of viruses and spyware. Every time you visit, that's where it's coming from. Now, I'm not gonna visit the page because then we'll have to do another cleanup, but I'd scrub your cookies from here and avoid it."

It was the site I used to track the human traffickers. How could it be giving me spyware without my knowledge, or the antivirus software not catch it?

"Hmm. And how do you know this?" I asked. When I glanced at Jemini, she seemed to have the same question, and looked a little skeptical.

"That's what you're paying me the big bucks for. Right, handsome?" She smirked at me once more, the lines of scars on her cheeks lifting with the smile.

Avoiding the question and then trying to charm me. I was young but not stupid. I put on a practiced smile and said, "Well, I guess. Speaking of…" I fished five one-hundred dollar bills from my pocket and handed them to her.

She looked at them but didn't take them. "Nah, this one's on the house. I mean, I should take it for having to endure that frisking from big red back there, but it's fine. You'll just owe me one. How about that?"

I didn't like that either. I wanted to see her again but not because I owed her. However, something told me she was holding back and I wanted to get to the bottom of it. "Here, this is my personal cell. Hit me up when you want to call in that favor, all right?" I scribbled down my number on a sticky note and handed it to her.

She grinned and stuck it into her pocket. "I will."

"If we're done, let me walk you out," I said.

She stood, and I inhaled that rosy citrus scent once more, memorizing it.

We walked out into the clubhouse and poor Venom was pacing like the expectant father he was.

I looked at my watch. "Only three more hours, man."

He stopped pacing and looked at me, then Rocky, then back to me.

"Statistically, the first baby takes about twelve to eighteen hours of labor before it's born. You'll get there in plenty of time, I'm sure." I used to think my brain was full of useless information. At least that one came in helpful this time.

Harlan went to his word tiles and touched *Thanks*.

Rocky made a noise. "Huh, clever. Who thought that one up?"

"Big red," Jemini replied sarcastically.

"Well, he's smarter than he looks." Rocky laughed, and I cringed.

"He's my fiancé, but thanks," Jemini deadpanned.

Rocky had the grace to look embarrassed. "Oh, shit, I'm sorry. I have absolutely zero social skills and no real filter on my mouth. It's why I stay inside most of the time." She offered a sheepish smile.

"It's cool. Thanks for your help today," I said, opening the door for her.

"No problem. Call if you need any more help."

With that, she walked out and disappeared into the night.

I closed the door and went to walk back to my office, but Jemini stood in my way, her arms folded across her chest, an eyebrow raised. "Did I interrupt something when I came back to the office with the news about Kalissa?"

I forced a straight face and feigned ignorance. "What? No."

A small grin forced her lips up. "I beg to differ."

"You imagined it," I replied, side-stepping around her.

Damn her and her witchy intuition.

7

FREAKS & GEEKS
Rocky/Devon

I flipped the sticky note around in my fingers. I had already inputted his number into my phone and shot him a text with mine so he'd have my non-burner phone number, but I was having a hard time throwing away the tiny yellow square of paper. What was wrong with me? A sentimental sap I was not.

The way his dark-blue eyes had searched mine that night he and Jemini had hired me to help them eliminate the malware on his computer was what I thought about as my eyes drifted closed each morning before I fell asleep. Then earlier, I got the call they needed more help, and I was, of course, happy to oblige. After all, I knew the problems they were having would be easy for me to get rid of. I wondered what Face would do if he knew I was the one responsible for the malware on the Nighthawks' computer system to begin with? The vampires I worked for owned that site on the Dark Web and they paid me very well to keep that spyware on the site to track anyone who visited it. So long as those Cash App deposits kept coming, I'd continue to monitor the site and keep the spyware active. I didn't have to tell Face that was where their viruses were coming from, but something about him made me do stupid things. He looked like he'd be a big, arrogant jerk, but he was the opposite. Polite and a little nerdy. Not really my type, but then again, I didn't have a type. I knew any chance at dating or love had been taken from me decades ago, so I avoided even thinking about it. The way he was looking at me earlier and that weird moment between us had just been my imagination. Nobody that hot would be attracted to me. Nobody *not* hot would be, either for that matter.

Looking the way I did, I stayed mostly inside and really had nothing else going on in my life. After I was turned, I took night classes to learn computer science and then pored over hacking articles on the Dark Web until I learned how to do the most sinister things to cyber systems. Chat rooms were filled with people just like me, looking to get in where they could fit in, since it clearly was not in the real world. If I couldn't be accepted amongst humans and fellow vampires, I would find my tribe online. After all, I could be anything I wanted to be on the internet. Right?

Unfortunately, my access to all things on the Dark Web had led me to a site where humans were kidnapping kids. I'd been horrified to learn there were real monsters in New Orleans doing terrible, sinister things, and I was tracking them closely. So close that I had got a drop on where two of them would be a couple of nights ago and had followed them. The text from one of my burner phones to the Nighthawks' and the FBI's snitch lines had been sent easily enough. The phone and its guts were then completely destroyed by fire before I threw it into the Mississippi.

My other burner rang with an unknown number, and I answered it. "Rocky."

"I got a job you might be interested in. Meet me at Zombies in half an hour," the male voice said.

"Who is this?" I asked.

I was met with silence as the call ended. Well, this better be worth my time. I had no idea who this stranger was. He hadn't even given me a description of himself.

My apartment in the Quarter overlooked Chatares Street, so I closed and locked my door, made my way down the stairs, and headed out on foot to Zombies, only a four-block walk. Pulling the hood of my sweatshirt tighter over my head, I walked quickly with my head down to the popular nightclub. I went straight up to the bar and ordered a beer, waiting for this stranger to arrive.

I didn't have to wait long. Not five minutes later a man walked up to me and asked if I was Rocky... my alias.

"Yes," I replied eyeing the strange, small vampire curiously. He wore a black trench coat, and his bald head was covered by a black ball cap.

He licked his lips and looked around. "I got a job for you."

I raised my brow, the bottle to my lips. "What kind of job?"

His gaze darted around the club again. "I need you to hack into something."

"You need to learn how to be more conspicuous, man. Looking around the club like this makes you seem suspect. Act normal."

His brown eyes went wide. "Okay."

"What's your name?" I asked the stranger, who was now inside my space.

"Joe," he replied. "Hey, what happened to your face?"

I ignored his question as I caught the attention of Theo and summoned him over.

"What can I do for you, Rocky?" Theo asked.

"Fifteen minutes in your office?" I asked.

He nodded. "Of course."

We followed him to the back office of the club, and I handed him a fifty-dollar bill before he closed the door behind him.

"Sit," I told Joe. "What can I do for you?"

"I need you to hack into the DMV and get me an address," he replied, still looking nervous.

"For what purpose?" I asked.

Joe cleared his throat. "Just need it is all."

"Are you a stalker, Joe?" I asked, crossing my arms against my hoodie.

He gasped. "No. I swear. I just need to know her address for… personal reasons."

"Who is this person?" I'd do just about anything for money, but

I didn't assist criminals, sexual deviants, or murderers.

He hesitated.

I pointed at my wrist where there was no watch. "Tick-tock, Joey."

Licking his lips, he finally replied, "I know you won't believe me, but she's my daughter. I was turned when she was just a baby and I had to leave her and her mom. I just wanna make sure she's okay. Watch over her. Ya know? With the rising crime here in the city... I worry."

I lifted an eyebrow. "So, you were turned when she was a baby and you stayed in the city? Nobody's recognized you?"

"I, uh, stay in the shadows."

Staring hard into his eyes, I analyzed him. He had no air of deceit and his gaze looked desperate and sad. Finally, I said, "Okay. It's two hundred upfront, and another three once I get you the info you need."

Joe relaxed and fished two bills from his pocket, then laid them on the desk. "No problem. And thank you."

I snorted. "Don't thank me yet." I went to the DMV's site and easily accessed their servers. "What's her name and date of birth?"

Joe gave me the information I needed, and I found her driver's license easily enough. I printed it out for him and handed it over. "The other three is due now."

After he slapped the bills into the palm of my hand, I said, "Pleasure doing business with you." I quickly wiped Theo's computer history and we left the office.

We went our separate ways, me walking down the sidewalk back toward the safety of my apartment. All I wanted was to get back to the computer to see what Parker was doing. I grinned to myself as I thought about his "club" nickname. It was easy enough to figure out how he'd acquired the nickname, but his real name had been on the gradation diploma from the University of North Texas hanging on his office wall, and I had tucked that little bit of info into my brain for proper stalking later. A simple reverse image search of his handsome mug I'd snagged from his driver's license photo had shown me all I needed to know about the guy. Hundreds of pictures popped up of him in various ads, and my favorite—a huge billboard in Southern California depicting him in his underwear not dissimilar to the famous Marky-Mark Calvin Klein ad from the nineties. Except Parker Lee Knight was so much sexier and gorgeous than Mr. Wahlberg could ever be.

My daydreaming had made for a quick walk back to my place. I sucked down a blood bag from the fridge before going back to my dark corner and checking the Nighthawks' computer system. Face accessing that site I managed had led me to the discovery of the vampire bikers who seemed to want to be the unethical cops of the underworld of this city. My obsession with them had been going on for months. Every time I witnessed or learned of a supernatural crime, I'd texted their lame anonymous tip line and they had always followed up with me watching from the shadows like some deranged stalker.

Maybe that was what I was. Because that would always be what I did. Hide in the shadows, stealing blood bags from the local blood bank because I was too hideous and frightening to feed from the abundance of blood whores in this city who got paid for their delicious human blood.

My phone rang with another unknown number. I answered, "Rocky."

"Hello, ma'am. I am currently in need of your computer assistance," drawled a male voice that sounded like he'd been alive, or at least existing, for a very long.

"Sure, what can I do for you?" I asked.

"I would like to acquire your services. I need you to gather some information on a subject I've been trying to find. I've hit a dead end and thought maybe you could help me find out more about this person through the use of modern technology and the internet?" he replied.

I smiled at his formal language. Definitely an old vampire. "Absolutely. When would you like to meet?"

8

BABY WOLF

Face

Thankfully, Bloome had been keeping in close contact with MyAnna about the baby. She wasn't even halfway through her labor when the sun started to come up and Harlan transformed back into his human form. He didn't even bother to shower—he put on his clothes, hopped on his bike, and sped to the hospital. It was then I felt comfortable enough to go upstairs and go to bed. I had been keeping him company. I wanted to be supportive and didn't want him thinking I didn't care.

After a blood bag, I lay down and fell asleep quickly, Rocky's beautiful green eyes the last thing I saw before sleep pulled me under.

I walked out of the audition stunned. Out of all the guys in that waiting room, I'd been the last to interview for the part and was told that I had been just who they'd been waiting for. I was instructed to come back tomorrow to begin photographing. They ordered me to get a haircut, teeth whitening treatment, and a fully nude spray tan. Hair cut above the ears and collar, and longer on the top.

Once I reached the lobby of the building, I searched on my phone for the closest barber. Thankfully, there was one a few blocks down and I could walk there. The wait was long, but I didn't mind, I liked to people-watch. I stared out at the bustling sidewalks full of people and hoped I would get used to it. I'd moved out here in hopes of becoming an actor but was told I needed to try modeling first to get my foot in the door. Back home in Texas, I'd found a photographer to do some headshots of me and then I'd Googled modeling agencies in LA. I sent my headshot off to every single one of them—over a dozen. I got three replies, with an invitation from them all to come to the city of angels at my own expense and audition for them. I apparently got lucky and landed the first one I interviewed for. I cringed when they said it was an underwear ad, but it was apparent I was going to have to get over whatever shyness I had real quick. They'd made me strip down to my boxers during the audition. Wasn't even sure why they called it an audition—I had no real talent except with computers, and apparently, very good genes.

After the haircut, which cost me much more than I planned, I located a tanning salon on the same street. I was stoked to find out I could whiten my teeth and get a spray tan at the same spot. Those were both expensive as well, and I hoped this job would pay me enough for all this ridiculously shallow upkeep.

The next day, I was nervous as I arrived at the building they'd told me to go to for the photo shoot. Bright lights and too much noise greeted me in a lobby with a pretty receptionist who instructed me where to go. Walking into the room, I was overwhelmed by all the large cameras, portable lights, and backdrops.

"Hello, Parker. How are you?" the older guy I'd interviewed with yesterday, Ellis, greeted me.

"I'm good. Nervous, honestly."

"Well, you look fantastic. Love the hair and your teeth look much brighter." A woman walked up to us holding a camera. "This is Lisa, photog extraordinaire."

I shook her hand. "Nice to meet you."

"Let's get started," she said, leading me to a large wardrobe room where clothes were hung up on racks. A tuxedo, a business suit, a pair of jeans, and a polo shirt hung on one hook. "Those are your clothes for the shoot. Start with the jeans outfit and come out when you're ready."

I nodded, taking the outfit and putting it on. The label told me it was very expensive, but they fit like a glove and were very comfortable. "No wonder people pay an arm and leg for this stuff," I muttered to myself as I slid on leather loafers and went out into the studio.

Ellis whistled between his teeth. "Very nice."

I had no idea what I was doing and was nervous that I would look stupid trying to make poses, but Lisa was very helpful. After three outfit changes, I thought it was done, but was told there were a pair of designer boxer briefs in a drawer, and I was to come out in them with nothing else.

And here I thought they'd changed their mind on the underwear photos. Oh well. I looked at the small white pair and slipped them on. Again, very comfortable, and admittedly, my ass looked amazing in them.

After a very uncomfortable photo shoot, I was told I could keep any of the clothes, except the tux, and they insisted I take the underwear. I took the three-piece suit, the jeans, and polo. I was handed a check for two thousand dollars and left the studio happy. I couldn't believe I'd made that much money for just a couple of hours of work that really wasn't work.

Two weeks later, I was walking down the sidewalk, on my way to another shoot, and almost shit myself when I looked up in horror at an eye-catching billboard on Hollywood Boulevard. It was me in nothing but the underwear I was ironically wearing today. I put my head down and walked quickly toward the studio.

I blinked my eyes open. I didn't regret doing those photo shoots but of course once the guys here caught wind and Googled it, I'd never lived it down. Shadow had printed out that ad and hung it in the breakroom. I'd changed all his passwords after that and didn't give them back for a week.

I slogged out of bed, brushed my teeth, and put on my gym clothes.

After my workout, I headed to the showers and scrubbed myself clean. I thought about what I was going to do now that I couldn't access the human trafficking site on the Dark Web any longer. I needed to find a way to keep tabs on them—it was my job. I promised Viper I'd keep him updated on the situation. Last I read, these people had been in Texas. It was only a matter of time before they arrived here. They seemed to have hit every major city, starting in Southern California and moving east. LA, Phoenix, Albuquerque, El Paso, Houston, Dallas. I didn't have proof they'd come here but had a strong feeling since we were the next largest city, and this town had a lot of shady-ass people. The problem was… I suspected they were already here due to the fact those two girls had been kidnapped. But how would I know if I couldn't access that site? Maybe I could buy a cheap laptop and use that without it being connected to our servers. If they put spyware on it, they wouldn't see much, just an anonymous, non-registered device looking at it. But then again… accessing that site took a lot of juice, and without all the power I needed, I didn't think I could pull it off. Dammit.

I was going to have to ask for Rocky's help yet again. I already owed her a favor, now it would be two. I dried myself off and dressed in my jeans, boots, white tee, and cut. I then pulled out my phone and saw a message on the group text: *It's a boy! Jameson Andrew Lahey* was captioned to a photo of a very wrinkly red baby wrapped in a blue blanket.

"Aww," I said aloud and typed out a congratulations. When I'd gotten up this evening, MyAnna had told me Kalissa still hadn't had the baby yet. Glad to see everyone was happy and healthy.

I stared down at the phone. Call or text? I looked at the time: 8:15 p.m. Did Rocky have a job, or was this computer help/hacking her only income? I wondered what she was doing right now. *Guess I'll find out.* I found her name in my contacts.

Me: *Hey, it's Face. You busy?*

Sixty agonizing seconds later, she replied.

Rocky: *Depends. What do you need?*

Me: *I need more help but I'd like to meet somewhere else outside the clubhouse.*

Rocky: *Computer help? Meet me at Zombies, Theo lets me use his office for business.*

Wow didn't know that. I was a little frustrated, though. Yes, I wanted to see what she thought I should do, but no, it wouldn't require a computer. I told myself I just needed computer help, but I really just wanted to talk to her. Be near her. Which so wasn't like me.

Me: *I would just like to pick your brain is all. No need for a computer. There's an all-night diner on Sixth, meet me there?*

Another thirty-eight seconds go by.

Rocky: *I know the place. I'll be there in fifteen.*

I responded with a thumbs-up emoji because I was lame and sucked at this shit.

After hopping on my bike, I headed toward the diner.

9

REVENGE OF THE NERDS

Face

I drummed my fingers on the tabletop and sipped water while I waited for her. It had been thirty minutes and she still wasn't there. No texts either. Just when I began to think I was being stood up, I spotted a hooded figure open the door to the diner. Breathing a sigh of relief, I waved her over.

She sat across from me, and her familiar rosy citrus smell drifted into my nose. "Hello, sorry I'm late. Couldn't get an Uber right away. Friday night and all."

"It's fine. You don't have a car?"

She shook her head. "No, I rarely go anywhere that isn't walking distance. Didn't see the use in paying for one, along with the insurance and gas. Car services are cheaper in the long run when I do need to get somewhere."

The server arrived at our table. "Hello, what can I get you?"

"I'll take a club soda with a lime," Rocky replied.

"Sure, hon," the server said, looking at her and doing a double-take before plastering on a fake smile. "Anything to eat?"

"Got a menu?" she asked.

The server used the pen to indicate a pile of menus against the wall at the end of our table and drawled, "They're over there, hon."

"Thanks," Rocky replied, grabbing one and looking it over.

I raised an eyebrow as I watched her silently.

She looked up from the menu. "What?"

"First, take the hood off. Please. Secondly, why are you looking at food? Are you seriously going to eat it?"

She slowly slid the hood down and looked around the café. Her long brown hair was tied to the back in two large braids. Small wisps of loose curls framed her face. I had to refrain from staring at her lips and instead held her green gaze. "No. I have a neighbor, single-mom type, and I bring her food sometimes. I feel bad if I go somewhere and don't order anything but drinks, unless it's a bar. So, I just get it to-go."

"Well, that's very noble of you. I'll go ahead and order something too, then. You can bring her mine." I grabbed a menu. "What does she like?"

She held my gaze for a while and said, "Honestly, I have no idea. I usually just order the special or something that I remember was popular, like spaghetti or meatloaf. It's been so long since I had food, I really don't know what humans like to eat."

"Rocky, how long have you been a vampire?" I asked, setting my menu down after I'd decided what to order.

She also set hers down. "So, my real name is Devon, and you can call me that. I use an alias for obvious reasons when meeting strangers. But if you tell anyone, I'll probably have to kill you."

I smiled. "That's a beautiful name. Thank you for sharing that with me. My lips are sealed though. Go on."

"Since the nineties, to answer your question."

I was born in the nineties. So weird. Still trying to get used to the immortality thing. "Thanks. I was just curious."

"What about you?" she asked.

I took a sip of the water then set it down. "I'm a baby. Only been turned five years. I was twenty-one, and I guess I'll… always be twenty-one."

"I was twenty-seven," she replied.

The server stopped by and asked if we were ready to order.

"Club sandwich, fries, side of ketchup," I said. "Strawberry cheesecake."

"Catfish platter with everything." Devon smiled at her. "And a slice of whatever pie is good."

"You got it," the server said, walking away.

"Kathy and the kids are gonna eat good tomorrow," she said with a grin.

I nodded. "You got that right."

"Thanks," she said, smiling. The scars stretched almost painfully-looking across her cheeks, but I quickly diverted my attention to her eyes so she wouldn't think I was staring too much at them. Or, God forbid, repulsed or in any way scared. "So, what did you want to pick my brain about?"

"I need to maintain access to that website on the Dark Web you told me to avoid. Just wanted to see if you had any ideas what I could do. I thought about using a cheap laptop with regular WiFi so if I got spyware it really wouldn't be too detrimental."

She shook her head. "You need a lot of bandwidth to access the D.W., handsome. That won't work."

Please tell me she is not going to keep calling me that!

"Since we're sharing today, I'm Parker, you can call me that if you don't like my club name."

"You definitely look like a Parker." She winked.

I cleared my throat. "Okay, any other ideas? I cannot compromise the club's network under any circumstances."

"Why do you need access to that particular site, if you don't mind me asking?"

I hesitated. "That site is run by human traffickers."

Her face dropped. "No, it's not. They just buy and sell illegal things. I've, uh, been on it before."

Is that what she really thinks? "You're right, they do. People. Mostly underage kids and young women."

She shifted uncomfortably and said, "Okay, well, what are you going to do about it?"

"They're not going to make it past New Orleans. In fact, I think they may already be here. We need to be a step ahead of them."

She cocked her head to the side and glanced around the restaurant. "Really? You're, what, just gonna kill them?"

"As long as we have proof, most likely. Nighthawks don't tolerate that shit."

"Leave it to the cops," she replied quickly.

The server brought our food and set it down in front of us. Devon and I wrinkled our noses at the smell.

"Should have just told her to bring it in to-go boxes," I said.

"Too obvious. We have to look like we're eating. Pick up a French fry and just hold it in your hand."

I obeyed. It was warm and greasy. She unwrapped her napkin, pulled out the fork, and held it in her hand.

"We did," I replied. "Sort of. To the supernatural cops. We got a tip on a kidnapping a couple nights ago. They sailed off on a speedboat and there was nothing we could do, so we called the authorities. We don't normally do that, though."

"The BSI? Right?"

I nodded. "Yes. There was already an AMBER Alert out for the girls so it wasn't something we could have handled internally anyway."

"Why didn't you just call the FBI?" she asked, tapping the bottom of the fork against the catfish.

"Two reasons. One, we have a close professional relationship with the BSI. They visit regularly to check up on us. Two, the anonymous tip we received stated the kidnappers were vampires. The BSI will have to handle it if that's the case. Though, what I can't figure out is how the tipster knew they were vamps. Made me wonder if they knew them."

"You can't trace the text?" she asked curiously.

I shook my head. "No, it's set up to be completely anonymous."

"You should change that," she replied. "I would."

"Trust me, after this, I'm strongly considering it, especially since this was damn near a life-or-death situation."

"Well, unfortunately, unless you want to just keep removing spyware, there's no other way to access that site without another elaborate setup."

"How many seconds do you think I have to access the site before the malware worms in?" I asked. I had to keep my eyes on hers to avoid wanting to stare at her beautiful lips.

"The site detects a visitor immediately, so it'll go to work with the bug right off the bat." She sat back in the booth and added, "I mean, I assume so."

I raised an eyebrow. "You don't know?"

"I'm good, but I'm not that good."

I bet you are.

Realizing I was at a dead end, I made a mental note to do more research on the Dark Web about this stuff, try to beat it at its own game without accessing that site. If I could just get a name of who ran it, I could work backward from there. "Okay, well, thanks for listening."

"How's the pregnant wolf lady?" she asked, her eyes sparkling mischievously.

I bit back a grin. "She's not a wolf, the baby is. A boy, born just a few hours ago in fact." For whatever reason, I pulled out my phone and showed her the photo.

She made a face. "They sure are ugly little things when they're born, huh?"

I almost spit out my water. "I don't think you're supposed to say things like that."

"My auntie used to tell me that when she saw an ugly baby, she would say, 'Oh, isn't he just the most precious thing you ever did see? Bless his heart.' Then you'd know she thought it was ugly."

I chuckled. "Gotta love those Southern aunties and their backhanded compliments."

She grinned. "You from the South?"

"Yes, grew up in a small town outside of Austin. You?" I asked, happy she was taking an interest in me personally.

"I'm from Alexandria, just north of here. Had to move away for a while, you know. Been back here about five years."

The server appeared at our table. "Wow, y'all not hungry or what? I was just about to bring the desserts out."

"Guess we got to talkin', but I need to go," Devon said. "Can you box it all up, including the desserts, and I'll take it with me for later?"

"Sure, hon."

After she was out of earshot, I looked at Devon. "So, is this what you do for a living? Side jobs for computer help? Or do you have a regular gig?"

She shrugged. "I have a few hustles that pay enough for rent and utilities with enough left over for toys."

My eyes widened. "What?"

"You know, new servers, maybe a fancy new monitor every once in a while. Gotta replace that chair every year or so as well."

I snorted. "You don't get out much, do you?"

Staring hard at me, she shook her head. "No."

In another bold move, I reached across the table and grabbed her hand. She flinched and looked at me, almost confused. "Thank you for meeting me. You've given me some things to think about."

She looked down at our hands and then back up to me. "Anytime, handsome."

As I was about to ask her to not call me that, the server set the food boxes down along with the bill. I snatched it up.

"You gotta let me pay for that. I'm taking all this food with me."

"No," I said, setting my credit card down on top of it. "I asked you here, I have no problem paying. And if you wanna know a little secret, I don't get out much either." I winked at her.

10

GIRL, INTERRUPTED
Devon

After Parker paid the bill, he got up and offered me a hand up, but I remained seated.

"I need to call the car service, so I'll just hang out until they get here."

"Nah, don't bother. I'll give you a lift."

A mild panic invaded my chest. I never let anyone know where I lived. "Don't you drive a motorcycle? Where will we put this food?" I stalled.

"Yes, and I can strap it to the back of the bike with the bungee. I've also got a backpack and we can put it in there if you want."

Shit, what other excuse could I come up with? I looked up into his ridiculous handsomeness and almost caved when he threw that charming-ass grin at me. Since he now knew my first name, I figured with his skills, he could easily find out not only my last, but where I lived. In fact, I was sure that was exactly what he was going to do once he got back to that warehouse they all lived in.

"Okay, I guess I'll take you up on that."

His lips twitched. "You sure? Took you long enough to decide. If you don't want me to know where you live, I can just drop you in the general vicinity if you're more comfortable with that."

It was like this dude could read my mind. I was beginning to think we were almost too much alike. "Well, I'm sure you're just gonna go on a search when you get back to your place anyway, so it's fine, you can drop me off at my building."

He chuckled and led me out the door. "Well, I wasn't going to, but since you already assume I would, I think I will now."

"Don't bother, the last name's O'Donnell. Then, you'll soon see where I live, and all your curiosity will be gone, and you'll have time for other things. Like figuring out how to access your favorite D.W. site without getting malware."

"Hop on, smartass," he said, taking the food from me. "Just sling one leg over." He grabbed my hand to steady me, and I felt a tingle rush up my arm at his touch, like I had in the diner. After I was on, he put the boxes on the back and hopped on the front. The engine was so loud I wanted to cover my ears. I lifted the hood over my head.

"What's the address?" he yelled over the noise.

I told him.

"Hold on tight to my waist," he instructed.

Slowly, I put my hands around his waist and pressed my front against his back. We drove through the city in silence, and when we neared my apartment building, I pointed to it. He brought the bike to a stop and put his feet on the ground to steady it. After killing the engine and putting the kickstand down, he helped me off.

"Well, thanks for the ride," I said, as he handed me the food boxes.

"First time on a motorcycle?" he asked with a grin.

"You forget I'm older than I look," I deadpanned.

"Well... do you need me to carry those up for you? Or help deliver them?" he asked.

I bit back a smile at the cute way he was stalling. "Nah, I think I can manage."

He stepped toward me and reached up one hand toward my cheek, like he wanted to touch me, maybe kiss me, but I turned my head and took a step back. "I... I'm sorry. Goodnight, Parker."

Turning away quickly, I rushed inside my building without looking back. I heard the motorcycle start up a few seconds later.

I set the food boxes in front of Kathy's door, knocked, and then went down the hall to my studio apartment. Once inside, I closed and locked the door and then pressed my back against it.

Well, that was the most social interaction I'd had in... forever. Was he really going to touch me? Kiss me? I was so out of the game that I didn't even know. All I knew was that I didn't want to be touched on the face. He probably thought I just didn't want him to touch me at all. That wasn't the case. It had been so long since I'd met someone I was attracted to, who was also attracted to me, and I had no idea what I was doing. *Sigh.*

I threw my hoodie onto the sofa and went over to my workstation. I smiled at the photo of Parker in his underwear ad I was using for the background on one of my monitors and brought up the server I used to access the Dark Web. After punching in several commands, I went to the website I maintained for these alleged human traffickers and took a good look around. I still refused to believe that was what they were. Parker had to be wrong.

There were several boards and sub-boards with titles like, *Makes You Feel Young Again* and *The Softer the Better*. I clicked on one and my stomach roiled in disgust. Photos of kids, from toddlers to teens, in various stages of undress, were featured inside the boards.

"What the fuck?" I whispered, hating myself for clicking on a photo of a completely nude teenage boy. The text was captioned with his age, price, and a link to contact. The boy's face wasn't shown but he did have some bodily bruises. I gagged and almost vomited up the club soda.

"God, Devon, you're such an idiot!" I chastised myself.

These people had approached me a few months ago for a "job." The only difference between this one and the others I did was this was completely online and anonymous, and I knew nothing about them. They stated they had a buy-and-sell site that had items they couldn't sell on traditional sites due to laws, and I figured it was probably drugs, alcohol, blood for vamps, stolen goods—even human organs crossed my mind. Problem was, it was too easy for me to take the job. I just had to infect the site with spyware, monitor it like once a day, and report back to them as to who had accessed the site. I never really took a look around it.

Shame on me.

"Fuck!" I said, standing up and swiping the keyboard off the desk where it clattered to the floor. I paced the living room floor with my thumbnail to my mouth. What was I going to do now? I couldn't keep working for these sick animals. My stomach was already in knots. I felt like I'd assisted them in ruining children's lives—hell, some of them might even be dead. I knew what happened to a lot of those kids. They were sold to abusive pedophiles and were sometimes even killed. Tears welled in my eyes.

I had to make this right.

I sat back down, picked up the keyboard, and put it back. First thing I did was find the Nighthawks' computer in the list of visitors and put a protection on it that would prevent it from getting malware so Parker could continue to monitor them. I knew I had to report this to the BSI since it was run by vampires, and it killed me that I couldn't shut it down yet. Once the authorities figured out who was running this site, I was going to try to bring this disgusting thing down with a crash, and then plant bugs all up in their shit.

My phone chimed, and I was reminded that I had a meeting in thirty minutes with the old-sounding vampire to help him locate someone. After a few more keystrokes, I grabbed my keys, phone, and hoodie, and headed out the door.

The bench was set under a canopy of trees next to the water. The moon's reflection on the river bobbed with the waves. I approached the bench with caution when I saw a man with his back to me, looking out over the Mississippi. There were very few people around at this hour.

"Gregory?" I asked from about five feet away.

He turned his head around and smiled at me. He looked to be about thirty, but I knew he was much older than that. "Yes. You must be Rocky?"

I nodded and approached him slowly, my hood over my head, my hands in my pockets. "Yes. What can I do for you?"

He patted the bench. "Come, have a seat. I don't bite."

I stayed rooted to the spot. "I do."

He threw his head back and laughed. "I don't mind."

Slowly, I approached the bench and sat as far from him as possible. I waited for him to answer my question.

"Well, aren't you a woman of few words."

"So I've been told," I deadpanned.

I craned my neck to the side to relieve the stiffness, and the moon lit up my face briefly.

"Oh, my. What happened to your face, dear? Are you all right?"

I smirked. "You should see the other guy."

He laughed again. "You're quite the character."

"Let's get to the matter at hand. I have work to do," I replied.

"Yes, well, down to business it is. I have a slight problem and I'm told you're the person who can help me. As I explained over the telephone, I've been trying to locate an individual and have hit a bit of a dead end. Can you help me?"

"Sounds like you need a private investigator, not a computer hacker."

He shook his head. "Well, I've had no luck with PIs, I'm afraid. I think this person has taken on a new identity. They've all hit dead ends."

This piqued my interest. I loved a good challenge. "Okay, tell me who this person is and why you want to find them."

"I don't see why the 'why' is important, dear. I'll pay you well to not ask questions. It's a personal matter, someone from my past."

I went to stand. "See, here's the thing, Greg. I don't do jobs for perverts, pedophiles, stalkers, or any other kind of deviants." *Well, apparently I did, but in my defense I didn't know.* "So if you're trying to find this person so you can do them harm, then I'm out."

He put his hand on my arm. "Please don't go. I promise I am none of those things." He removed his grip when I stared down at it and folded his hands in his lap as I sat back down. Staring out at the water, he said, "When I was turned almost a hundred years ago, I stayed with my wife and children for a few months, but then I just had to leave. I wasn't eating food and couldn't go out in the daytime. Plus, I was afraid I'd slaughter them all when I got hungry. My wife, and everyone we knew, didn't understand. I stayed in the shadows and kept tabs on them occasionally, but about five years after, I was forced to move out of my hometown under circumstances beyond my control. I assumed my wife had died after decades passed, but I could never find record of her death. I now believe she may have been turned and I want to find her. If for nothing else than to tell her how sorry I am for leaving her and the children in the dead of night without so much of a note."

Damn. If this guy was telling the truth, that was some sad shit. "I'm not sure I'll be able to find her, especially if it was that long ago. There were no computer records until the late nineteen seventies, and even then, some have been destroyed due to fire or water, and with no internet until the nineties, those records are gone."

He pulled a photo out of his suit jacket pocket and handed it to me. "What about that facial recognition software? I've been reading a lot about it. It's fairly precise, is it not?"

I took the photo and looked at it. It was a grainy black and white picture of a woman staring unsmiling into the camera. She had long dark hair, fair skin, and plain features. "I'd have to do some serious cleaning up on this photo and then, yeah, I could try some software. Please text me everything you know about her. Full name, date, and city of birth, children's names, parents' names, everything. I'm going to have to keep this, but I promise I'll give it back."

He smiled. "So, you'll help me?"

I nodded. "Yep, Greg-o. I'll help you."

Gregory grabbed my hand and patted it with his other. "Thank you, Rocky."

11

DEVIL IN THE DETAILS

Face

On my way back to the clubhouse, I went over and over the interaction with Devon in my mind, almost obsessively. I couldn't control wanting to touch her, and she very clearly did not want that. Much to my disappointment, I realized that I was probably in the friend zone and would have to accept that we were going to only be friends and that was it. As much as I didn't want that, I knew I'd take her any way I could, as long as I could be around her.

After parking my bike in the lot, I wandered inside the clubhouse and saw everyone standing in a crowded circle, looking at something. I went over and saw Bloome showing pictures of baby Jameson on her iPad. They all looked the same. Fat baby wrapped in a blue blanket sleeping. I chuckled and went to head toward my office.

"What's up?" Phoenix asked me.

"Nothing. Just gonna get some work done."

"You're a workaholic," he said.

I shrugged. "Nothing better to do, I guess."

He folded his arms across his cut. "You need a woman."

Turning my back on him and walking away, I said, "No, I don't." There was only one woman I wanted, and I couldn't have her, so if that made me a workaholic, so be it.

I pulled my phone from my pocket and set it on the desk before taking off my leather jacket and hanging it on the back of the door. I picked up the phone to see I had a text.

Rocky: *I figured out a way to let you access that site without the spyware. Try it when you're ready.*

I set the phone down and excitedly accessed the Dark Web, quickly finding the site. I carefully entered and kept my proverbial fingers crossed that no malware came through. So far, so good. I navigated around the site and saw that there were more boards than before. Gritting my teeth, I clicked on the ones that appeared to be newer and saw even more children up for sale. I wanted to shut this site down so badly, but I couldn't until these guys were caught. It would take a lot of work to shut it down, anyway, and I wasn't sure I had the skills. I began to wonder if I shouldn't just call the FBI. It would be the right thing to do. My stomach churned in disgust.

I picked up my phone, changed her contact name to Devon instead of Rocky, and replied to her text: *Thank you, worked like a charm. You're a genius. I had a nice time tonight by the way. I hope I didn't do anything to scare you away. I'd like to be friends.*

Then, I texted Viper: *Can I see you in my office?*

The phone chimed.

Devon: *You're welcome, I'm glad it worked. I had a good time too. And no, I don't scare that easily ;)*

"What's up?" Viper poked his head in.

"I was able to get back into the human trafficking site. Look." I pointed to all the message boards and showed him the children for sale.

His face went murderous. "Sick fucks. When are they coming to New Orleans?"

I shook my head. "I don't know, but I can't, in good conscience, let this site stay up. Kids are getting hurt every day. You good if I tip off the FBI?"

Viper looked at the screen again, his jaw bunching. "Yeah, do it. Enough of this bullshit. I'd like to kill them myself, but we can't wait around, just hoping they'd be in New Orleans soon. I know you said they've been moving the operation east, but it's been weeks. Enough's enough. Do it."

I felt an enormous weight lift off my chest. "Thanks, boss. I'll do that tonight."

Knowing I had Devon to thank, I decided to text her.

Me: *It's definitely a human trafficking site. Did you look at it? I'm calling the FBI. We can't wait and hope they come to New Orleans. There are new posts every day. They have to be stopped.*

Her reply was immediate.

Devon: *NO! DON'T CALL THE FBI!*

What the fuck?

Alarmed, I picked up the phone and dialed her number. She didn't answer until the fourth ring, which told me she was unsure about answering. "Hi, Parker."

"Give me one good reason to not call the authorities, Devon."

She hesitated, then sighed. "Because they're vampires, and I work for them."

I pulled the phone away from my ear, looked at the screen, then put it back to my head. "I'm sorry. I thought I just heard you say that they're vampires and you fucking work for them."

She was quiet and replied, "I did. They hired me to add and remove the spyware. But—"

Anger burned in my chest. "What the hell, Devon? Who *are* you?"

"I can explain."

"Ya know what? It doesn't even matter. This just goes to prove that you don't know who you can trust. I can't believe I trusted you."

"Would you just listen to me for a minute? I didn't know it was a human trafficking site, I swear. I only maintained the malware portion of it."

I scoffed. "Sure, you didn't. I hope they paid you well because

I'm shutting that site down after I call, well, now the BSI. Goodbye, Devon, or Rocky, or whoever you are." I ended the call and tossed the phone onto my desk.

God, I couldn't remember the last time I was this furious. No wonder she was able to implant and debug the malware so easily—she'd probably written the code that created it. What was the purpose of her helping us then? I was so confused. I needed to clear my head and decide how I was going to proceed.

I snatched my phone from the desk and went up to my apartment. Changing into my workout clothes, I left the clubhouse without saying a word to anyone. Everyone looked at me curiously as I stormed out and slammed the door.

I'd been on this treadmill for forty-five minutes and had no plans to stop. My phone had buzzed with texts, but I refused to look at it. I needed a break and to clear my head.

I considered myself a pretty intelligent guy, but this, I just couldn't wrap my head around. Devon helped us with the malware problem, knowing it would just come back. Right? No, that wasn't right. She didn't know we were visiting the trafficker website until she came to the clubhouse and saw it in my history. But she had known we were visiting it because she was in charge of the site's security, so to speak. Did she know it was actually us? Had she hacked into my system? Yes, she had, through the use of spyware. Then when we asked her for more help because it came back, she was so easily able to remove it because it was her malware to begin with. After our conversation earlier in the diner, she went home and was magically able to let me back into the site. Because she'd removed the bugs. She had told me it wasn't a human trafficking site. How could she not know? It was unbelievable, and I felt like such a fool for trusting her. I couldn't believe I actually thought about trying to pursue something romantic with her.

You idiot.

I pushed myself harder, fueled by anger, and after an hour had passed, I hopped off, grabbed my phone, and sat in the locker room to cool down. I certainly wasn't as sweaty as I should be, but I did feel a zip of energy and my body was warmer than my resting temperature—which was pretty cold.

It was at times like this I wondered how my life had ended up here. This wasn't the plan for my future. I was supposed to become a famous actor and party my life away on yachts with beautiful people, not become a creature of the night. But I doubted any vampire had wanted this life, I and knew I certainly didn't. However, I was partly responsible for the monster I'd become. I closed my eyes at the regret that haunted me every day.

After two years of modeling, I was making enough money to live in one of the nicest high-rise condos in LA. I was invited to parties every night and only turned them down if I had an early shoot or big job the following day. So far, the auditions I'd attended for film roles had all been busts. I had enrolled in acting classes and told myself if I didn't get a job in the TV or movie industry in three years, I would go back to Texas and get a college degree. I was pretty good with computers and technology; it came naturally to me, and the money was good.

A nice, older gentleman, who was a known film producer, was at a party one night. My agent, Erik, introduced us.

"Parker Knight, this is Martin Russo." Erik looked at Martin. "Parker's a model, he's done quite a few prints and billboards over the past two years."

I shook his hand and he smiled wide at me. "It's great to meet you. Love your work. Especially the billboard ad."

The billboard I'll never live down.

"Thanks," I said, smiling. "That was my first modeling job."

His eyebrows shot up. "Really? Looked like a pro to me." Then, he winked.

Okay, that was weird, but everyone in this town was a little bit off, in my opinion. I just played the game so I could get what I wanted.

"Well, that's very kind of you."

We chatted for a while, and as we were parting ways, he offered me his business card. "Call me if you're interested in auditioning for film roles. Ever done any acting?"

I shook my head. "Honestly, no. But it's why I moved to LA."

His face brightened, the fine wrinkles around his eyes crinkling next to the silver at his temples. "That's great." He smacked the side of my arm and with another wink and pointed at the card in my hand. "Hey, hit me up, all right?"

I held it up. "Will do."

I never got the nerve to hit him up, though. Weeks later, he ended up contacting me, and it was the night my life was changed forever.

I shook my head to clear the memory.

After showering, I headed back to the clubhouse to keep myself busy before I did something stupid, like go to Devon's and throttle her.

12

SCARS AND STRIPES

Devon

"You're so stupid, Devon! You should have just let him call the FBI. What would it have mattered?" I yelled while staring at my face in the bathroom mirror. "Dammit!" I stormed out and sat at my workstation. Leaning back, I tapped my fingers on the armrest of the chair. What was I going to do now? It wasn't like those payments were keeping me afloat, but they were a good portion of my income. I was so angry I hadn't investigated the site better.

When they'd first hired me a year ago, I did take a look around, saw the names of the message boards, but never clicked on them. They just appeared to be items for sale with cutesy titles to get people to click. After a while, I never even went on the site, I only visited the servers to collect the data from the spyware and then logged off, usually too wrapped up in some other hack I was busy with at the time. Then, I discovered the Nighthawks, and they became my complete obsession. I saw their group texts and would feel like I was reading some thrilling live-action role play. I would leave the apartment to hide in the shadows, watching whatever they were doing at the time. I almost got caught once, a few weeks ago when they were trying to rescue who I now know is Jemini. It was so exciting to watch them leap into action, but the kidnappers spotted me as they'd gotten out of the car to do the exchange for that necklace they wanted, and I'd bolted.

When I got the call from Mack, a guy Jemini used to work with—a human I'd met by doing a job for him—I had been so excited. Because I'd spent decades hiding and being socially awkward, I'd never figured out how I could meet the bikers. I was jealous of their group and how close they were with each other. I'd hacked into the cameras inside that nightclub they owned and used to watch them interact with each other. Since being turned, I'd never had that. I didn't even have any friends except the ones I made online—and even they didn't know the true me. If I hadn't met some of them to chat with, though, I probably would have died of loneliness.

Going out with Parker had been the most social I'd been in... I couldn't remember how long. I felt so stupid now. He was so angry, and I knew he'd never speak to me again. I was a fool for even thinking he was interested in me. Why would someone like that want to be with someone like me? He was the beauty and I was the beast. I'd obviously misread any signals he'd given off and never felt more humiliated in my existence. It was clear I needed to just stay indoors, only going out to meet clients for jobs or steal blood from the blood bank. It was where I felt safe, and I could keep from getting hurt.

Deciding I better get all the information of the visitors to the site before it got shut down by the cops, I searched for new visitors and found fifteen of them. I quickly gathered their information and put it into the spreadsheet I'd created. The one I sent over to the owners of the site every week. It was detailed, with IP addresses, any names or business names I could track down, frequency of visits, and dates and times. I would hand it over to the feds if they asked for it, but I wasn't going to volunteer it, because that would lead them to a whole bunch of questions that I had no interest in answering. I'd have to disappear and start over, and I didn't want that. I'd just settled here five years ago and liked it. The nights were more alive than the day, and there were plenty of shady characters around who needed less-than-ethical computer help.

After that, I began doing a search for Gregory's wife. I opened up Photoshop, spent an hour cleaning up the photo as best as I could, then loaded it into the facial recognition software I'd stolen from an Israeli government agency. While that scanned millions of faces, I pulled up the text he'd sent me with her personal information. I entered it all into LexisNexis. I didn't think I would get much, but a possible match popped up. Same first name and date of birth, different last name, different year. I excitedly pulled up her driver's license photo and loaded it into the facial recognition software. It was a 98% match. It seemed Greg's wife had been living as Sue Ann Johnson in Minneapolis. A quick background check showed she had no children or spouse, and owned a bakery there called *Sue Ann's Southern Sweets*. How apropos. I giggled and printed everything out for him. That was the easiest thousand bucks I'd ever made.

"Cha-ching! Show me the monayyy, Gregory!"

An alert from my police scanner caught my attention. "Attention all radio units, we have a possible sighting of two individuals, wanted for kidnapping. They were spotted on the east bank of the Mississippi disembarking a red and white speedboat. Two White males, dark clothing, most likely armed. All available units respond. Proceed with caution."

The temptation to stay home was too great, so I shoved all the documents and photo into a large manilla envelope and sealed it. Then, I grabbed my hoodie and cell phone and walked out the door.

13

VAMPIRE PROOF

Face

I sat at the computer staring at a blank screen. I was in no mood to work.

"What's up, buttercup?" Jemini asked, walking into the office carrying a coffee mug reading *Not Today, Satan*.

"Nothing," I replied grouchily.

"Who pissed in your Wheaties this fine evening?" she asked with a snort.

"Gross," I replied.

She laughed. "My dad used to say it to my mom when she was in a bad mood."

I ignored her question. "Why you so chipper?"

She sat in the chair next to me and set the mug down. "Because I think Gabe's gonna propose."

I lifted an eyebrow. "Oh yeah? What makes you think so?"

She shrugged one shoulder. "The browser search history on the communal computer."

"And?" I asked, mildly intrigued because I wanted to get my mind off of Devon.

"And... someone went searching for 'reputable jewelers in New Orleans.'"

I chuckled. "How do you know it was him? Maybe MyAnna wants a new necklace or something? Vane spoils her."

"Nope," she replied smugly. "I made everyone create a username and password for the computer. Gabe was logged in when the search was made."

"Well, I won't offer congratulations yet, but just promise me you'll act surprised if he pops the question. He's a little sensitive, I think. He'd get his feelings hurt if he thought you were expecting it."

"Don't you worry your pretty little head about that. I've got mad acting skills."

Laughing, I asked, "Did you tell Jermaine?"

"No. I literally just found out and you were the first person I ran into, so I had to tell someone."

"Why were you looking at browser history, anyway?" I asked, typing my password into my own computer to get started on my work night.

"Because I'm nosy," she replied.

"You need a hobby," I grumbled.

She placed a hand on my arm, and I looked up into her light-colored eyes. "Seriously, Parker. What's wrong? You've got this... this dark aura around you." She made a circle with her finger around my face.

"You can see auras now?" I asked, lifting an eyebrow.

"I've always been able to, but I didn't know what they were. Bloome's helping me."

I shook my head. I thought it was silly, but I wasn't a witch so what did I know?

"Just tell me. I'm a good listener," she plead.

"Turns out Devon's been keeping a secret from us," I spit out reluctantly. I hated talking about my feelings.

She furrowed her brow. "Who's Devon?"

"Sorry, Rocky. Devon's her real name."

"How did you find that out?" she asked.

I smirked. "Because I'm nosy."

"Okay... but what secret has she been keeping?"

"The malware, the spyware... we got infected because of her."

Jemini stood up and put her hands on her hips. "What the hell? She planted it?"

I cleared my throat and pulled up the Dark Web website. "Yes and no. Turns out she works for the pieces of shit who run this site." I turned the monitor around to show her the human trafficking page.

"That's how she was so easily able to get the malware removed from our system. Damn, that sucks. I thought she could be trusted. How did you get it out of her?"

"I told her we were calling the FBI. Then she panicked and told me not to call them. Like all-caps screaming texted me. So I called her. She eventually answered and confessed that she was responsible for the malware, and that—get this—the site is run by vamps. She gets paid by them for this crap."

"How could she, or heck, anyone, knowingly assist human traffickers?" She shook her head. "There are some sick people in this world."

"She claims she was told it was a buy-sell website for illegal items. Didn't know that meant human children. Look at this sick shit." I clicked on a listing titled *Chocolate, Vanilla & Brown Sugar – Why Choose?* Three kids, most likely under ten, of different races, were sitting in chairs wearing only underwear. Their faces were cut out of the photo and there were prices for each one, and a discounted price for all three, listed in the caption.

"Oh, my God." Jemini put her hand over her mouth, her eyes filled with tears. I hadn't shown her anything up until now because I didn't want anyone else having to try to unsee this trash. "That's horrible. We have to shut this site down now! Can't you give it a big, fat, ugly virus?"

"We can't shut it down." I sighed. "We have to leave it up so the authorities can see it."

"But they're vampires, Rocky said. You can't call the FBI," she replied, staring at the screen.

I closed the site and said, "BSI. They'll have to take care of it somehow. I hope they have good computer people working for them. I've already documented as much as I could and was going to finish tonight. I wish I knew a way to keep the site up but keep people from visiting it."

"There is a way, but you'd have to be the one who built the site, or at least have admin access to do it." She blew out a breath. "Does Viper know?"

"He knows it's a human trafficking site and told me to call the FBI. He doesn't know this newest stuff with Devon. It all went down before I went to the gym earlier."

She looked at me, sympathy coloring her features. "I'm really sorry, Parker. I know you were wanting something with her. You really liked her, I could tell."

"It's fine, I don't have time for romantic bullshit right now, anyway. I'm just glad I found out when I did."

Just then, the police scanner caught our attention. We listened to an announcement about the kidnapping suspects being spotted.

"Crap, let's go," I said, grabbing my jacket and phone and heading out to the clubhouse.

"Where's the fire?" MyAnna asked as Jemini and I rushed out of the hallway.

"Viper, where's he at?" I asked her.

"Cobalt," she replied, pointing toward the walkway.

"Thanks." We rushed into the crowded club and found him sitting at the bar talking to Ally.

I leaned in to speak into his ear over the noise. "Boss, the men who kidnapped those two girls were spotted on the east bank. NOPD is on their way. What do you wanna do?"

"You and I will head down there alone. Too many bikes will draw their attention."

"We could take the van?" I suggested.

He nodded. "Good idea. Grab Phoenix too, then. Let's go."

After parking in a nearby lot, the three of us piled out of the van and walked slowly toward the flashing blue and red lights at the edge of the river. There were three police cars, and uniformed officers milled around. Two men wearing all black were cuffed with their hands behind their back, sitting on a nearby curb.

I pulled out my phone and brought up the anonymous text we'd received last week, along with the photo. It was hard to see but they looked very similar to the two suspects in handcuffs. "They're not vampires, are they?" I asked the other two.

Viper stared at the scene. "Hard to say from here. They could easily break those cuffs and blitz out of there if they were. Not to mention, they would have never let the police catch them. So, I'm gonna say no."

"I wonder why the tipster said they were vamps?" I wondered aloud.

"Because I knew you wouldn't respond if you thought it was just a human problem."

We whirled around to see Devon standing there, her hands in the pockets of her hoodie.

"Hello, Rocky," Phoenix said.

"How ya doin', big red?" She smirked.

He chuckled. "Like I haven't heard that before."

"*You* texted in that tip?" Viper asked, narrowing his eyes.

They were being too nice to her, but they didn't know what I knew.

"Why don't you tell them how we got all that fucking malware on our computer, Devon?" I seethed.

"Devon?" Viper asked.

She ignored me and looked at Vane. "Yes, that's my real name. I use Rocky as an alias for jobs."

"Why would you trick us into responding to a human problem?" I asked.

"Because you guys are the best. The FBI would have taken too long." She shrugged.

"If they're human, why the hell didn't you just stop them?" Viper asked. "You're a vampire, you could take them."

She shook her head. "Nah. I'm a lover, not a fighter."

I tried not to smile at the remark and mentally kicked myself for thinking how cute it was.

"What's this about malware?" Viper asked.

Devon glanced at me from under her hood.

"Take the hood off," I snapped.

She narrowed her eyes at me. "No." She looked at Viper. "I was hired to put spyware on the human trafficking page to track visitors to the site. When I was called to help y'all, I didn't know it was going to be *that* site he'd been visiting that caused it or I would have stayed out of it. It wasn't until he showed me his browsing history. Lots of viruses and shit on the D.W., so I, at first, figured it came from elsewhere."

"Yeah, but you had spyware on our shit. You could have tracked that he was visiting that site, right?" Viper asked.

"Yes," I responded for her.

She half-grinned. "No, Face here was removing it too fast."

"Why would you work for such human filth? You just do anything for money, or what?" Viper asked, his hands on the hips of his jeans.

"First off, they're not humans, they're vamps." She pointed

toward the scene. "Those are humans. Totally separate from the guys I work for. Secondly, I didn't know it was used for human trafficking. I thought it was a buy-and-sell type site for illegal stuff, like drugs and blood for vamps. Other shit you can't sell online legally."

"I don't know jack about computers, but how do you run a website and not know what's on it?" Phoenix asked, his arms crossed in front of his cut.

Devon blew out a breath. "I don't *run* the website. I implant malware into visitors to the site's computers. I didn't read what was on it, which was my mistake and I'll own that. It was Parker who told me what kind of webpage it was. He told me he was calling the FBI and I had to tell him not to, then fess up. Since then, I've been cloning pages and saving them to a secure system, so if you want to call the supernatural feds, I've got most of it documented. It needs to be shut down ASAP, though."

Listening to her explain it that way, my anger began to wane. If she was telling the truth, then she really hadn't known. She had been careless, stupid, and money-hungry, though, and that was not cool.

"I'll call them right now," Viper said, pulling his phone from his pocket and punching some buttons on the screen.

"I'm gonna go see if I can eavesdrop on the cops," Phoenix said, then walked off.

She watched them walk off then looked up at me. "I'm sorry, Parker. I didn't mean to deceive you. I realized my mistake and was going to just get rid of all the garbage on the computer for you and then leave it at that. In fact, I have to thank you for pointing out the true nature of the site. I was careless and should have done more digging before taking the job."

Her green eyes were glossy with regret, and she looked so apologetic, and I was starting to soften at the sincerity in their depths. "It's fine, Devon. Can't change what happened. Did you tell them you were quitting?"

She shook her head. "No, figured once the feds shut down the site I won't have to."

"Lower the hoodie. Please," I asked, exasperated.

Reluctantly, she used both hands to push it off her head. Her hair was down in long brown waves, and she immediately pulled some of it to curtain her face. I grabbed her wrist gently and lowered it. "You don't have to hide from me."

She looked down at the connection, and I pulled my hand away.

"Can you shut the site down yourself?" I asked.

She shook her head. "I could probably keep it up and block users from finding it, but to shut the whole thing down, I don't think so. Not even with a nasty trojan horse virus. They'd just contact me to get rid of it, anyway."

"Do they know who you are and where you live?" I asked, concerned.

"No, never met them or talked to them in person or on the phone. They just Cash App me the payment and I use a burner phone to contact them."

"Smart," I murmured. "But how do you know they're vampires?"

"They told me they were and made me prove I was one as well."

I narrowed my eyes. "How do you prove that without meeting them?"

"I had to send them a picture of my fangs and answer questions only real vampires would know."

"So, they have your picture then?" I inquired.

"Just my mouth," she replied quickly. "And a short video of me cutting my arm and watching it heal."

Viper walked up to us and pocketed his phone. "BSI are on the way. I told them to meet us at the clubhouse so you could show them everything."

"Good idea," I replied.

Phoenix returned and said, "They're pretty sure those are the kidnappers. Two suits from the FBI showed up. They're taking the suspects and plan to interrogate them on the location of the girls. They're human."

"I hope the girls are okay," Devon murmured.

"Well, we should go," I said, hating that I'd rather spend time with Devon than go back and work because I was still angry at her, which I would analyze later.

"Bye," she said as we walked back toward the van. Before climbing into the back, I looked to where Devon had been standing, and she was gone.

14

GOODBYE, SWEET HUMANITY

Face

Agent Nolan Bishop looked at the computer screen, his look of horror mimicking Agent Shields's. "There are too many sick perverts in this world," he said, shaking his head. "I've seen enough. Close the window."

I minimized the page and said, "Now you know why we can't call the FBI. You guys have to find these vamps."

"We still have to call in the FBI. They have more manpower to rescue the kids. We'll take care of the vampires when and if they catch these guys. In the meantime, we have to treat it like a human problem and locate those children ASAP," Shields commented.

"Understandable," I agreed.

The agents took the chairs in front of my desk while Viper and Jemini stood in the corner.

"How long have you been tracking these people? This site?" Agent Bishop asked.

"Over a month. I've been watching their moves. They started on the west coast and are moving east, using the southern highways. They were in Texas last I checked. The plan was, we were going to take care of them once they reached New Orleans," I answered. "But then those two girls were nabbed, and we thought they were already here. Turned out that was a separate case."

"*Take care of*? Like kill? When you thought they were human?" Shields asked.

"Human monsters," Viper said. "You feds have too much red tape."

"So, you were just going to 'take care' of them like you did those humans a few months ago who kidnapped your wolf?"

Viper groaned. "Are we still on that? We've been over this. What's done is done."

"I had to write a very creative report for my supervisors after that. And I only did it as a one-time favor. Criminals or not, you don't harm humans. You call us or the police," Bishop said.

"Back to these assholes," I said, pointing at the computer. "How long is it gonna take the FBI to shut down the site?"

"Not long," Bishop said. "I don't know anything about computers, but we have some brilliant minds in DC. I'll tip them off and they'll get to work on it."

"And if they catch the vamps?" I asked.

"We have a liaison between the FBI and BSI who discreetly notifies us if they have a supernatural case or suspect. Don't worry, we won't drop the ball."

I wasn't sure how good that made me feel. "Look, I have a contact who's been cloning the site, so once it's shut down, hit me up and I'll send you the files."

"Who's this contact?" Agent Bishop asked, his pen poised above his notebook.

"An independent contractor. She knows her way around the Dark Web," Jemini answered.

"We'll need to speak to her," Shields added.

I shook my head. "She won't talk to cops."

Why am I protecting her?

She huffed and stopped typing on her phone. "Why not?"

I shrugged. "I can ask, but no promises."

The agents headed for the door and said, "Contact us as soon as you find out."

"I'll walk you out," Jemini said.

After they were gone, Viper asked, "Are you going to see if Devon will talk to them?"

I was conflicted. I wanted an excuse to see her again, but I knew she wouldn't talk to the BSI, not to mention she couldn't tell them anything we hadn't already. It was in the feds' hands now.

"I'll see," I reluctantly replied.

"Keep me posted," Viper said, leaving the office.

The sun was due to come up, and I was starting to get tired. I shut down the computer, went upstairs, stripped off my clothes, and fell asleep.

"I can't believe you've never done acting before. You were such a natural today," Martin said as we sat around a large circular grouping of sofas inside his mansion. There were tons of beautiful people milling around, talking, drinking, laughing, and snorting cocaine and Xanax off the tables and counters using rolled-up hundred-dollar bills. I'd just gotten done wrapping up a commercial for a pharmaceutical company, where I was cast into the role of a high school student who was praising the efficacy of the medicine they were peddling while playing basketball. It didn't require great acting skills, but it was something for the résumé.

"Well, thanks, Martin. It wasn't as stressful as I thought it would be."

He was sitting a little too close to me and making me uncomfortable. I could also swear he was flirting with me, too, but I remained polite. I needed to keep in good graces with these people. I couldn't bring myself to flirt back with him, though, for fear of giving him the wrong idea.

I'd recently grown out my hair a little bit, and it now was below my ears and touched my collar in the back. Martin reached up and moved some of it out of my eyes. "Commercials are easy. It's big film that requires memorization of lines and a lot of commitment."

I swallowed hard and wished he'd stop touching me. "I could see that." I picked up my drink and took a sip to see if he'd move out of my space. I extended my elbow out a little bit and it worked, he backed up.

"So, I wanted to let you in on a little secret, Parker," he said, still staring hard at me, making me want to squirm.

I swallowed the disgusting champagne. I couldn't believe that stuff cost eight hundred dollars a bottle. "Yeah? What's that?"

There was nobody else on the couches, but he still darted his eyes around a bit and lowered his voice. "I've got this drug that is out of this world. It's rare and nobody knows about it but a very select few. Wanna give it a try?"

"No, thank you. I stay away from drugs. I don't even really like to drink, honestly." I set the champagne flute down as if I was proving a point.

"No, this isn't some street drug or mood-altering shit. It's life-changing, shit, Parker."

That did not sound very appealing. "No, Martin. I'm good. Really."

He stood up, grabbed my hand, and made me stand. "C'mon, just let me show you."

I felt like I had no choice, so I followed him. I was hoping he wasn't going to try to force me to suck his dick or something, because while I'd do about anything to make it big, I drew the line at sexual favors. Man or woman. I was determined to make it on my own merit and talent.

We entered a large master bedroom in the back of the massive house. It had fancy shutters that were drawn up, where the view of the grassy, sprawling yard and swimming pool was on display, the moonlit foothills behind it.

I stood in the doorway and watched as he removed an oil painting of a woman and set it on the floor. Behind it was a safe built into the wall. He punched some buttons and the device beeped before he opened it. Pulling out a small box, he then set it on the nightstand and opened it. Encased in dry ice was a small vial. Curiosity got the better of me, and I wandered close to get a better look.

"What kind of drug requires dry ice?" I asked, pointing to it.

He held it up between his index finger and thumb. It was red, a little frozen, and looked like blood. "Do you ever wonder why everyone in Hollywood is so beautiful? How they all stay young?"

I shook my head. "No, I never wondered. Plastic surgery has come a long way. I figured they were doing treatments and surgeries."

"Well, some certainly do. But a lot of us have taken this. It keeps us youthful. How old do you say I am, Parker?" he asked in his slight Italian accent, piercing me with a cool brown stare.

"I... I don't know, Martin. I don't like to guess people's age. It's rude." There was no way I was going to insult this guy who was practically my ticket to fame.

He chuckled, his skin crinkling at the corners of his eyes. "C'mon, you can't hurt my feelings."

I stared at him, then said, "I don't know, forty-five?" I actually thought he was more like late fifties, but I didn't want to insult him in case he wasn't.

He laughed again. "I'm ninety-seven years old, young man."

My eyes widened. "No, you're not."

"Yes, I am. Unfortunately, I wasn't introduced to this magic potion until I was in my mid-fifties. But I won't really be aging much more after this, and I'm immune to diseases and viruses. It's amazing."

I didn't believe a word he said and was sure he had probably taken some kind of crap before I got here. "Well, that's pretty unbelievable," I replied, not sure what else to say.

"Don't you want to stay beautiful forever? Never get sick?" he asked, staring at me in the eye with such intensity, I found it hard to look away. I was starting to feel a little lightheaded and figured it was the champagne since I rarely drank.

"I... I don't know about that. I still look like a kid sometimes, hence the commercial I was cast in today," I replied. Hell no did I want to be twenty-one forever. The only appealing thing about the so-called drug he was offering was the immunity to disease and virus. Still, I wasn't sure he was even telling the truth.

"You won't be sorry, I promise you. There's just one little catch, though," he said, sitting on the bed and patting it for me to sit next to him.

Here we go. I obeyed and put my hands in my lap. "What's that?"

"I'll need a bit of your blood. It has to be mixed with this elixir to work properly."

Staring at him in revulsion, I said, "Absolutely not."

"It won't hurt. Just a little from your wrist." Why I hadn't noticed it before I wasn't sure, but I looked down and saw a metal cap over his index finger. It had a sharpened point at the end and looked like some kind of macabre thimble.

I pulled my wrist away. This was getting weird and I just wanted to leave. "I think I need to go." I went to stand, and he pushed me back down with surprising strength I didn't think he'd have for his age.

"Don't go. Please. I have so many plans for you. I just bought an action movie script that you would be perfect for. Leading role. You have my word, Parker."

My eyes went wide. "You think after one commercial I can get a leading role? No way."

He nodded and smiled again at me. "I'm the producer, I cast who I want."

"That sounds amazing," I said, getting excited at the thought.

"Just drink this, okay? It'll make you strong and healthy. Then, I'll make you rich and famous beyond your wildest dreams."

I licked my lips and looked at the vial. The way I saw it, this guy was full of shit. No way did I believe he was 97. So, I had nothing to lose by taking it. Even if I got high or something, it would wear *off and I would have appeased him so I could get that movie role.* "O... okay. I'll do it."

He clapped his hands and smiled. "Perfect. Now, give me your wrist."

I pushed the sleeve of my sweater up to my elbow and held it out for him. He used his sharp thimble to slice horizontally across my wrist. I hissed in pain. He dribbled my blood into the vial, and I watched as his eyes kind of glossed over. He clamped his mouth shut as if he was trying not to keep something in. Once he had as much as he wanted, he put the stopper back on and handed me his handkerchief from his pocket square. "Hold that on there."

Pushing the cloth onto my wrist, I watched as he shook the vial, and then pulled the stopper off. He handed it to me. "Drink it down in one shot. Like tequila or whiskey."

I smelled it, wrinkling my nose. "This is blood."

"Mixed with magic," he whispered, the corners of his lips tipping up as if he had a secret.

Furrowing my brow at the strange comment, I forced a smile and with a shrug said, "Bottoms up." It tasted awful and coppery, just like blood would, and I handed it back to him with a gag.

He set the vial on the nightstand and grabbed my hand. Pulling the handkerchief away, he began to lick the wound. It was gross and weird. "What are you—" I couldn't finish because my stomach cramped up something fierce, and an awful flash of raging heat began to race through my veins. I cried out for help and Martin laid me on the bed. I tried to protest but I was in too much pain.

What the hell is going on! *I screamed inside my mind.*

It wasn't long after when the darkness found me, and I was no longer human.

15

BEAUTY AND THE BEAST
Devon

Two days later, I sat at my workstation. I logged into the server for the disgusting site to collect the data. I knew if they were watching me, and I didn't act like business as usual, they'd get suspicious. Except it wasn't there. Had the feds taken it down that fast? If so, I was damn impressed.

Just then, the burner phone I had charging on the desk lit up and vibrated. I picked up to see a text from the vampires who owned the site.

V Boss: *Why is the site down? Get it back up immediately, Rocky!*

Me: *I didn't take it down. I was just about to text you because I noticed it too.*

There was a two-minute pause before their next reply and if I could sweat bullets like a human, I would have been.

V Boss: *Did you tell anyone about this site, Rocky?*

Why did they keep using my name? Creepy.

Me: *Of course not. Let me see what I can find out and I'll get back with you.*

V Boss: *You have one hour.*

Me: *It's going to take longer than that. And don't threaten me, asshole.*

I never talked to them like that, but I had them by the balls right now. Obviously, their computer guy or whoever set up the site couldn't figure it out.

I got no reply after that.

Picking up my regular cell phone, I dialed Parker's number.

"Hi, Devon," he answered.

"Hey. Sorry to bother you, but—"

"You're not bothering me."

I smiled. "Good to hear. Can we meet? I have a problem."

"Actually, I was just about to call you, anyway. I also have some questions. Do you want me to pick you up or can we meet someplace close by that you won't have to Uber to?"

"Let's just meet at Zombies," I replied.

"I'll see you in ten," he replied. "Bye."

I smiled and ended the call.

After walking the four blocks, I saw Parker was outside sitting on his motorcycle looking at his phone. He wore a white V-neck T-shirt and his leather Nighthawks vest. His arms looked huge and bulged against the sleeves.

So hot.

"Hey," I said, walking up with my hands in my pockets.

"You wanna go inside or talk out here?" he asked, pocketing his phone.

"Inside is better," I replied, looking around. The texts from the vampires had spooked me a little.

Theo was behind the bar talking to the bartender with an electronic tablet in his hand. "Hey, Theo," I said, walking up to the bar with Parker.

"Hey, how are you, Rocky?" He looked to my right. "Face, how's it going?" They shook hands.

"Can we use your office?" I asked.

He fished a key from his pocket and handed it to me. "Help yourself."

I held up the key. "Thanks."

Parker chuckled and said, "Come here often?"

I shrugged as we reached the door and I put the key in the lock. "I told you, he lets me meet clients here sometimes. I throw him a few bucks and he's good with it." We went inside and I closed and locked the door behind us. "I can't very well conduct business at my apartment."

"Why not?" he asked.

"Are you crazy? I don't need these whackos knowing where I live."

He shook his head with a smile. "Paranoid, much?"

"Yeah, pretty much," I said, nodding. "I don't have a bunch of big, strapping men to guard me while I work."

He lifted an eyebrow. "Cute. But you're a vampire. Aren't most of your 'clients' humans?"

"It's about fifty-fifty."

His beautiful lips tipped up in a grin. "Haven't you learned how to defend yourself? Do you work out?" Then, he leaned forward and used vampire speed to flick the hood off my head. "Don't make me do that again."

I ignored the thrill that gave me and resisted the urge to pull my hair in front of my face. "I don't have time to work out, nor do I like the stares I get when I do. I took some self-defense classes when I was human, don't really remember them, though. I've never had to get physical with someone."

He lifted an eyebrow and his lips twitched. "Is that so?"

The sexual suggestion wasn't lost on me, and I felt my cheeks flush. "No."

"Not in thirty years, you've never had a scuffle with anyone? Been threatened by hunters? Nothing?"

I shook my head. "No, I stay inside, period. In fact, this past month is the most socializing I've done in probably a decade."

He nodded and was quiet for a minute. "Devon, are you happy living like that? Are you content and satisfied with your life?"

Of course I wasn't. I hated the isolation, but I hated the way people in public treated me more. So I was stuck. I simply replied, "What did you want to meet me about?"

He sighed at my non-answer, and said, "Feds want to talk to you."

My eyes widened. "What? You told them about me? Why?"

"What's the problem? You said you wanted to help. Weren't you planning on sending those cloned pages to them?"

"Yes, but anonymously! The last thing I need is the feds being onto me."

He blew out a breath. "You *are* paranoid. You can talk to them and not give them your real name. Either way, it would be the right thing to do. Tell them what you know."

"I don't know any more than you do, so why can't you just tell them?" I asked, holding back a whine. "I don't exactly run a legal business here, you know."

"I already did, but they want those files and for you to tell them everything you know about these vamps."

The thought of talking to the feds made my stomach churn. "How about I give you the info and you can pass it along."

"I don't like it. You should do it," he replied.

"I'll think about it," I said, already knowing I wasn't going to be doing that.

He nodded. "Okay. Your turn. Why did you want to meet?"

I pulled the burner phone from my pocket, put in the passcode, and handed it to him. "They texted me this earlier."

He glanced over it then looked up at me with those beautiful dark-blue eyes. "They think you took the site down or know who did?"

"I think they're bluffing. They only hired me for the malware portion. They obviously have their own hacks running the site and know damn good and well I can't take it down without direct access."

"Yeah, but maybe they thought you put a bug in there to shut it down," he suggested.

I hadn't thought of that in my panic. "That's true, I guess. What should I do?"

He sat back in the chair and stared at me. "Are you scared, Devon?"

That was a loaded question, so I shrugged. "Yes and no? I'm pretty well protected, I don't even lease the apartment under my real name."

"Do they know where you live?" he asked.

"I don't think so. When I gave them the burner phone's number, it had a New Orleans area code and they asked if I lived here. I told them no, and how stupid that would be to use a burner with the area code where I lived. It was sort of a reverse psychology I'd tried to pull since I was stupid when I activated the phone and forgot to ask for a different area code." It was true, I still felt foolish about that type of dumb mistake, but there was nothing I could do about it now.

"I think you should come stay at the clubhouse," he said seriously. "I mean it."

"What? No way, I don't need bodyguards. I'm fine. I can take care of myself." I was acting tough but was secretly thrilled he was concerned about my well-being. I would feel so awkward and out of place there, anyway. I'd seen the women who lived there. They were all gorgeous and I was an ugly freak.

His jaw bunched in annoyance. "Not yet, but I have a feeling these vamps, whoever they are, are going to be downright furious when they realize they aren't getting their site back. Once they find out the cops are involved, they're going to look for someone to blame."

"Why would they blame me, though? I've done nothing to make them suspect me—"

I was cut off by Parker standing up and grabbing me by the hand. "Come on."

I stood but pulled my hand from his. "No. I don't need protection. I'm—"

Gasping as I was shoved against the door, I couldn't protest when his lips came crashing down on mine. They were soft, and with his hand gripping the back of my hair, he controlled where my head went. I kissed him back and hoped I was doing it right. I was so rusty that I literally couldn't remember how to make out with someone. I threw my arms around his neck and groaned when his other hand went protectively around my waist and pulled me flush up against his hard body.

I felt his tongue lick the seam of my lips and I opened up, allowing him access. Soon, both our tongues were dueling as our lips moved against each other's and then pulled away. Parker turned his head to the other side and kissed me again, his tongue slithering with mine. Pure arousal shot straight to my core, and I wanted him to rip my clothes off and fuck me right here against the door. Bold even for me, I pushed his leather vest off his shoulders and then reached down to his belt buckle as his hand left my waist and traveled up my stomach to my chest. When his fingers brushed my breast under my shirt but over my bra, I whimpered, feeling like I was going to have an orgasm right then.

Parker broke the kiss and stared into my eyes, panting. "Fuck, I want you."

"I want you, too," I said, excitement swirling in my stomach. I hadn't been laid in... I didn't even know.

But was it just sex I wanted? Yes, I definitely wanted to get some skin-on-skin action and let someone give me an orgasm for once. That toy could only do so much for me.

"Let's—"

A loud knock cut him off. "You guys done in there? It's almost closing time," Theo shouted.

"Yeah, we're done," Parker called out, shrugging his vest back up and buckling his belt.

I put the hood back over my head and used my hair to hide my flushed cheeks and swollen lips.

Parker opened the door and I handed Theo the key and a fifty-dollar bill. "Thanks, Theo."

We left the back room as Theo chuckled knowingly. I wanted to die of embarrassment.

As we reached the parking lot, Parker pointed to his motorcycle. "Get on."

Now that the lust had cleared, I folded my arms across my chest, "No. I'm going home."

"You are so stubborn. Why don't you want to come to the clubhouse?"

I smirked. "Are we going there to fuck?"

His eyes widened. "No, that's not what I meant. We don't have to do anything you don't want to." He stepped toward me and put his hand up to my face. I flinched back. "Sorry," he said. "I forgot."

I stepped up, grabbed his hand, and put it up to my cheek. I leaned in to his touch. "I'm sorry. It's a reflex."

He rubbed his thumb over my scars, and I had to mentally tell myself to stand still and not shrink back. "Do they hurt?" he whispered.

I blinked up at him. "Not at all."

Leaning down, he kissed me again, only this time it was soft and slow, unlike before. After pulling away, he looked down into my eyes. "Please, Devon? Just for a couple of nights?"

My resolve was faltering. "I don't know…"

"I won't sleep if I think you're in any kind of danger." His lips tipped up in a ghost of a smile, and I folded like a lawn chair.

"Okay, but I have something I have to do first."

His eyes bounced back and forth between mine. "What is it?"

"I have to finish a job. I owe a guy some information. It'll only take a few minutes."

Parker brushed some hair from my face. "That's fine. I'll go with you."

I shook my head. "No, my clients expect complete secrecy and discretion. I'll meet you at your clubhouse when I'm done."

"You don't have a car, and it's not walking distance."

Laughing, it was my turn to put my hand on his scruffy cheek. "I'll manage. I promise I'm not lying. I'll be there. I'll text you once I make the delivery so you'll know I'm on the way."

He hesitated, and finally said, "Fine. But I'm driving you back to your apartment."

"I can live with that."

After he dropped me off, I grabbed the manila envelope I'd forgotten to deliver to Gregory a couple of nights ago in lieu of the excitement down on the east bank. I'd apologized for standing him up, stating I had an emergency, and rescheduled for tonight.

I looked up at the half-moon and the clouds that now covered the sky, realizing it was looking like rain. I pulled the hood tighter over my head and walked toward the park. Once I arrived, he was waiting faithfully on the same park bench.

"Hello, Rocky."

I sat down and pulled my hood down. "Hi. I think you're going to be pleased with what I found."

He opened the envelope and read the printouts. He stared at Sue Ann's driver's license, and then looked at me with unshed tears in his eyes. "This is definitely her. I can't believe I forgot about that birthmark on her neck right there." He pointed to a small mark peeking out from her blouse in the photo. He chuckled and said,

"Sue Ann's Southern Sweets? Oh, that's so her. The woman was baking treats constantly." Gregory looked up at me. "I can't thank you enough. I owe you a debt of gratitude."

I laughed. "Nah, but a thousand bucks will do."

He reached into his inside jacket pocket, pulled out a money clip, and counted out cash. I put it into my pocket and stood up. He pulled me into a hug unexpectedly. "Thank you, Rocky. I can't wait to see her. I hope she'll have me!"

"You're welcome. Good luck, and pleasure doing business with you!"

We parted ways, and I walked back toward my apartment whistling the tune to "When The Saints Go Marching In." Yes, I was actually whistling. I hadn't been this happy or in such a great mood in... well, I couldn't remember when.

As I was rounding the corner to my apartment, someone sucker-punched me in the face, and I fell to the ground in a heap, seeing stars and then nothing at all.

LOST AND FOUND
Face

Looking at my watch for the umpteenth time, I realized she wasn't going to show. How could she lie to my face like that?

"What's wrong?" Shadow asked as I paced the breakroom. I realized I hadn't eaten in a couple of days and was waiting for the microwave to beep. Then I realized it already had, like five minutes ago.

I glanced up at his huge frame then pulled the mug out of the microwave. I took a sip. It was lukewarm, and I scowled but drank it anyway. "I invited Devon here tonight and she freakin' stood me up."

"You invited her here for a date? You shouldn't be such a cheap-ass, man. Take her to the movies or something." He chuckled.

"No, I think she's in danger."

"Why?" he asked, frowning.

"Did Viper fill you in on everything?" At his nod, I continued, "Those vamps she worked for suspect her of taking their damn human trafficking site down. She tried to tell me she could protect herself, but I know she isn't that strong." I sipped more blood. "So, she finally relented, but said she had a job and then she'd be right over after. That was over an hour ago."

"Maybe the job took longer than expected?" Shadow asked. "You call or text her?"

I set the mug down and looked sheepishly at him. "Not yet."

"Don't play games, call her. Maybe she couldn't get a ride or something."

He had a point. It was Saturday night in New Orleans, so maybe all the car services and taxis were busy. I pulled the phone from my pocket and dialed her number. It went straight to voicemail as if it was shut off. "Call me when you get this, Devon." I ended the call and shot her a text with the same message.

"No answer. Straight to voicemail, in fact," I said to Shadow.

"That's not good. But, if she thinks she can protect herself, then you shouldn't worry. She's a vampire."

I shot him a look. "She's not a very good vampire."

"So you have this need to protect her? Hmm. You know what that means, right?" He ran his fingers over his beard and pierced me with his gray eyes.

I rinsed the mug and put it in the dishwasher after listening to MyAnna complain the other night about it. "Listen, I'm not gonna lie and say I wasn't hoping for something else. I kissed her earlier and things got a little... heated. She seemed so into me, and I was so sure she'd show after she did her little side hustle. Now, nothing."

"Either she's ghosting you or she's in trouble," Bloome said, startling me as she walked into the breakroom and put her arms around Shadow's waist.

"Do you ever not eavesdrop?" I asked, staring at the redhead.

She laughed and looked up at Shadow. "What do you say, babe? Am I ever not nosy?"

"No, you always are," Jemini said, coming in with her twin brother trailing behind her.

"Bloome's nosier than Jem, and that's saying something," Jermaine said, laughing.

"Houseful of hens," I murmured, making my way toward the door to go sulk in my office. The least I could do was try to trace her phone, see where she was. I was sure I'd find she was at her apartment.

On my way to my office, I bumped into Viper.

"You good?" he asked after seeing the look on my face.

I explained the situation, and he said, "Something about that doesn't seem right. But she has been deceitful before."

Frustrated, I muttered, "Yeah." I continued down the hall with Viper telling me to hit him up if I wanted any help.

Sitting at my desk, I brought up the cell phone provider's website and considered what I was doing. I could hack in, find the location of her phone, and figure out where she was, just to placate my ego and help me get over the fact she'd rejected me. Or... I could just leave it alone and tell myself to get over it and stop obsessing. I bounced a pencil off my mousepad repeatedly and stared at the screen. Then, I checked my phone for missed calls or texts. Nothing. I briefly contemplated getting on my bike and driving to her apartment, except the problem was—I didn't know which unit was hers. She'd used an alias to lease it so no way to run that info either. I'd have to sit on my bike and hope she came out.

"This is insanity." I shook my head. "This is why me and relationships will never mix. I don't have time for this crap! And now I'm talking to myself, for fuck's sake."

I clicked out of the cell provider's website and went to work on a new anonymous text line we were going to use that would allow us to track the tipsters. Except every time I even thought about Devon, my traitorous dick would twitch in my pants until I had to think about anything else.

I sat in the now-closed Cobalt Room for church. I was in no mood to be around people. Hours had passed and not a peep from Devon. What a cock tease. No, scratch that. What a heart tease.

"We've come to a decision. Andy's club name will be Eagle. He's our legal eagle and is as sharp and keen as the rare bird." Viper presented Andy with his cut with *Eagle* on the patch. Andy—Eagle—beamed with pride as he shrugged it on. "Thanks, man." He pulled Vane into a man-hug.

"Thanks for taking me in. Y'all are really growing on me. I haven't felt family like this in a long time. I'm loving the camaraderie and brotherhood you have going on here. I've never been a part of something like this. I hope I can serve you all well while I'm here. If any of you run into legal problems, I'm your go-to. Don't ever hesitate. All right?"

Claps erupted and I joined in as well so as to not be rude. I liked Andy and was glad for him. My mood was just in the toilet. I had the nerve to call the house ladies hens when I was acting like the biggest one in the club right now. I needed to get a grip.

"Next order of business tonight," Viper started. "I received word from the BSI that the human trafficking site Face and Jemini were monitoring was shut down already by the feds. Not only that, the FBI managed to extract the location of the two kidnapped girls from the human suspects and are on their way to pick up the girls. Apparently, they had already been taken to the Dominican Republic to a buyer who paid thousands for them."

I shuddered. Disgusting fucking humans.

"Next, Venom, Karissa, and baby Jameson are now home at Karissa's house, and all are doing well. Once they feel up to it, they'll bring the baby by for a peek. Until then, please give them some time and space to adjust to their new life."

A few squeals by the hens could be heard.

"Lastly, we believe the threat is gone to our servers, so you're good to use your cell phones and tablets freely and turn the location services back on, if you'd like. Any questions?" Vane picked up his bloody wine and took a sip.

When no hands went up, Viper adjourned church.

As I was making my way back to my office, Jemini fell into step with me. "What do we have going on tonight? Anything you need help with?"

"Just working on the new text program," I muttered.

We went into the office and Jemini stood staring at me with her arms folded. "What's wrong?"

Deciding she'd just get it out of me anyway, I knew there was no use lying or glossing over what was going on. "Devon's ghosting me."

She sat in the chair next to me and said, "What do you mean? She's just not responding to you?"

"I met up with her earlier tonight to let her know about the BSI situation and how they wanted to talk to her, and we had a... moment."

She grinned. "What kind of moment?"

"Kissing and shit. I'm not going into detail, but you get what I'm saying... then she tells me the assholes who were running that disgusting site basically threatened her and accused her of getting the site taken down. She of course denied that she was in any danger and there was no way for them to find her, as they didn't even know her real name or where she lives, but I still didn't feel right about her being alone. So, after much persuasion, she agreed to come back here to the clubhouse for safety. She said she had to deliver some documents for a job she had, and she'd be right over. Never showed. Phone goes straight to voicemail."

Jemini's brow furrowed. "Hmm. Sounds like she's in trouble. Why don't you track her phone?"

I turned in my chair and looked at her. "I was going to, but it felt too stalkerish. If she doesn't want to see me, then whatever. I'm not going to get all in my feelings, but she could at least respond to my text. Ya know?"

She shook her head. "No. I can feel it, Parker. Something's wrong. I saw the way she looked at you and that moment you two had when I walked in on y'all the other day. There's mad chemistry between you two. Like, it almost makes me uncomfortable to be alone in a room with you guys, it's that strong. I don't think she's ghosting you. I think something happened to her. What if those guys caught up with her?"

Now, I was becoming alarmed. Jemini's intuition was always spot on. "Okay, fuck it. Let's do it. If not for anything but peace of mind for me. If her phone's still at her apartment, then I'll know she just doesn't want anything to do with me." I pulled up the cell provider's website, typed in her phone number for the username, and used my password-guessing software to try to log into her account.

"Problem is, even if her phone shows it's at her apartment, that doesn't necessarily mean she's there too. What if they kidnapped her?"

"Ugh, seriously? What is it with this club and all the kidnapping drama?"

She pointed at the screen. "How did you know she used that particular cell provider?"

"I did a search of her phone number and Google told me which cell provider was attached to that number. Easy."

I had no luck with the password-guessing software so it must be a complicated one. "No luck. Let me try something else."

I hacked into the police department's servers and punched her number into their cell tracking software. I only had about ninety seconds before it booted me out, so I bobbed my knee nervously, waiting for it to locate her number.

"Ah. There it is. It's at 187 Chatares Street," Jemini said.

I frowned. "That's her apartment complex."

She put a hand on my arm. "Like I said, doesn't mean anything. Just go down there, make sure she's okay. And if she is, tell her to go fuck herself." She shrugged.

I bit back a smile. She rarely cursed.

"And if she's not, call the calvary and the guys will help you find her."

I was so conflicted. Did I really want to do this? It felt too needy and creepy. "I don't know. God, I hate this stuff. This is why me and relationships do not mix. It's easier to stay single."

"It's easier, but it's not rewarding. Being in love with your other half and having them by your side is worth every misery, soul scar, and heartbreak you've ever endured, because once you've found your soulmate, you can't imagine a life without them. It becomes a seamless journey as easy as breathing." She had that dreamy, faraway look in her eye.

I scoffed. "I don't believe in soulmates."

"You will. Now, get." She shooed me out of my office and then took my seat behind the desk.

I killed the engine and hopped off my bike. The main entrance to the apartment complex had no lock or code, and while it was convenient for me, I didn't care for the lack of security with Devon living here alone. Yes, I was mad at her, but I wouldn't ever not care for her well-being. The office was closed, so, looking around briefly and seeing nobody, I used vampire strength to break the doorknob. I left the lights off and crept around to the filing cabinet. There was a computer, but I was going to try there last. I hoped they kept paper records.

I pulled the metal filing cabinet's handle, and it was locked. I yanked harder and broke the lock. Using the flashlight app on my phone, I rifled through the files. They were organized by apartment number, not name.

"Dammit." I didn't even know what floor she lived on. Then, I remembered she told me she'd rented the apartment under an alias. It took me fifteen minutes, but I did locate a Devon Smith who leased apartment 302. I pocketed the phone and left the office before sprinting up the stairs.

I knocked on the door. "Devon?" I pressed my ear to the door and heard absolutely nothing except the humming of her electronics and refrigerator.

I tried the handle, and it was unlocked. I became immediately alarmed. Nobody as paranoid as Devon would leave the door unlocked, home or not. I pulled the buck knife off my belt and slowly crept inside. "Devon?"

The apartment was small but neat and organized. A large workstation was set up in the corner with a desk containing four mounted monitors, a printer, and a bunch of external hard drives and modems. A back bedroom with a bed and dresser was the only bedroom there. In the closet were lots of hoodies on hangers. This was obviously her place.

I went back out into the living room and punched the space bar on the computer's keyboard to wake the computer. Very complicated screens of windows even I had trouble deciphering were on three of the screens. The other had no windows open on it, with a picture of a beach as the background

"I'll look at this later," I said to myself.

I searched the entire apartment for her cell phone and couldn't find it. "What the hell?" I said, running my hand through my hair. I left the door unlocked but closed it all the way and went back downstairs. After walking out of the building, I looked both ways down the street. People were walking around, cars drove by, and nothing seemed out of the ordinary. I went around to the side of the building, where an alley separated this one from the next. On the ground was a cell phone. It was up against the wall and blended in with the color of the building. I bent down and saw blood next to it. It was still a little tacky, so I put my finger in it and sniffed it. Vampire blood mixed with a whisper of her rosy-citrus cent. I then picked up the phone and wiped the dirt off on my pants, flipping it over. Its protective case depicted a popular video game, and I knew it was hers. Of course, the device was locked with a biometric lock. So unless I had a copy of her thumbprint, I wouldn't be getting into this phone quickly.

I looked up and down the street again. Obviously, something terrible had happened to her and I wanted to punch something. If I wouldn't have been such a tool and waited hours and hours to try to find her, whoever took her wouldn't have gotten such a long head start. Because I knew deep down, she'd been kidnapped, and it had to be those assholes from the website.

17

VAMPNAPPERS

Devon

I screamed in pain as I grabbed my nose and snapped it back straight. That fucker had broken it, I could still taste the blood on my lips. One of my captors, wearing one of those white tragedy theater masks and a hoodie, came rushing into the small room they held me in.

"The hell are you screaming for?" he barked.

"Tell me what you want with me. Huh?" I replied.

After I'd come to, I found myself on this boat. The below-deck room they held me in had no way to see to the outside, so I had no idea where we were. We could be floating on the Mississippi River or in the Bahamas. I had no idea how long I'd been out.

"Keep it down in here. Boss will be here shortly, then we'll be questioning you." He slammed the door and locked it from the outside.

I waited until I heard his footsteps pound up the stairs before pulling out my burner phone. After I'd been knocked out cold, they must have found my regular cell phone in my back pocket and took it. They didn't think to search me further because I had this one in the inside pocket of my hoodie. I had three-quarters of a battery left but it was going to drain fast because it was constantly looking for a signal. I had no bars.

To make matters worse, I didn't have anyone's number programmed into it. I should have memorized Parker's number but never got around to it. The only numbers in here were the contacts from the jobs I'd done, and of course the human trafficking dickheads. I remember Gregory telling me he owed me the world. Well, I didn't need the world right now, I just needed a small favor from him. My hands were tied with rope in front of me, but they hadn't chained me to the bed or anything. I walked around the room and held the phone up to the highest point, trying to see if I could get a signal. There was no WiFi on this boat either, I'd already searched. Not that it mattered, this phone only made calls and texts. It wasn't a smartphone because I didn't feel like paying for two plans. It was one of those prepaid things.

I typed out a text to Gregory as I constantly checked the door. I hoped maybe I'd get lucky, and we'd get a second or two of service wherever we were headed, and it would go through eventually.

Me: *Gregory, this is Rocky. I hate to ask but I need a favor. I've been taken by some men and they took my other phone that had all my contacts in it. I need you to go to the Cobalt Room, it's a bar near the Quarter, and ask for Face or Viper. Tell them I've been kidnapped and I'm on a boat or yacht somewhere. I have no idea where tho. Pls reply if you get this, and don't call this number, text only. Thanks.*

I hit send and just prayed it would go through. I also hoped Gregory was still in New Orleans and not in Minnesota reuniting with his long-lost wife.

I paced the room in a circle, thinking about Parker. He must be so pissed off at me right now. I was sure he thought I'd stood him up. I'd told him I'd be right over. Would he even go looking for me or just assume I'd ghosted him? I thought about his face... the blue of his eyes and those full lips... they had been so soft but commanding. The way his hands roamed my body and gripped my hair while we kissed. How he didn't care about my scars and touched my face like they weren't there. Tears welled in my eyes and rolled down my cheeks. I hadn't cried in what seemed like years. I'd never had anything make me feel this deeply since I'd been turned all those years ago. I wasn't crying because I had been kidnapped. My heart was breaking at the thought of never seeing Parker again. I hadn't even spent that much time with him but had begun to believe I was falling in love with him. And now he probably hated me, and I was going to be killed by these horrible traffickers before I could tell him. I pulled out my phone and sent another text to Gregory. I noticed the first one hadn't gone through yet, it was pending.

Me: *PS – if you do get ahold of Face, tell him I love him.*

I hit *send*. If I somehow made it out of here, and had to face him after such a confession, well, I'd have to come to grips with the possibility he didn't feel the same. But if I didn't make it out, at least he would have known my feelings.

I wiped away the tears and forced myself to think of something else. Like how I was going to get out of here. Truth be told, I hated vampires. After I was turned, I wanted to burn down every one of their homes, cars, and places of business. I walked over to the bed and lay down, trying to force myself to stay awake. It didn't work, though, because I could feel the weight of the impending sunrise and that always made me sleep like I'd been drugged.

I checked my reflection one last time before grabbing my purse and heading out the door. Once I reached the strip club, I parked in the back and made my way through the employees' entrance.

"Hey, Devon," Mace, the bartender, called out.

"Hey, what's new?" I asked as I set my purse and sweater behind the bar. Nights were starting to get a little chilly here in New Orleans, and I was a wuss when it came to the cold.

"Nothin'. You ready for tonight? We're gonna be slammed since Ginger and Bunny are up tonight." He used the glass he was cleaning to indicate the stage where the ladies were practicing their routines.

I chuckled. "I know. Put on the extra short skirt for some good tips," I said with a wink, shaking my hips.

He whistled between his teeth and gave me the once-over. "You get it, girl."

Laughing, I did my usual preps for the night and once the doors opened, I was busy from the minute they opened until three a.m. at last call, and only endured five ass-grabs and three butt slaps while serving cocktails. Exhausted, I counted up my tips and helped Mace and the other bartender clean up. My feet were screaming from the three-inch heels I'd worn all night, so I changed into the flats I'd thrown into my purse. I lifted my long hair out of the way and then shrugged on my sweater.

"Where's Benny?" I asked. He usually walked me to my car because a previous customer had been stalking me. He'd left me threatening and sometimes graphic, perverse notes on my car. Even mailed them to the club. I'd reported it to the police and even had a restraining order against him, but the guy always came sleazing around. Benny and the other bouncers would always get rid of him, but I didn't feel safe walking to my car alone. None of us girls did.

"I'm here," Benny said, his huge frame practically taking up the doorway. "Ready?"

I nodded and adjusted my purse over my shoulder.

"So, are you almost done with school?" Benny asked as we crossed the large lot. I'd parked next to the dumpsters to try to hide my car so creep-o stalker wouldn't see it, but it never worked.

"Yeah, gonna change my major, though. I don't think I want to teach anymore. I'm taking an interest in computers. Can't stay off that internet, it's like a shiny new toy."

He chuckled. "It is a shiny new toy. I can't be bothered with that computer stuff, it's all over my head. Can you get a degree in computers?"

I shook my head. "I don't know, I have an appointment tomorrow to go talk to a guidance counselor. I didn't see anything in the school catalogue about it, though."

"You're smart, I'm sure—"

I looked up at him to see why he'd stopped talking. The tip of a bloody knife was poking out through his throat. He was grappling for it, but soon his eyes rolled back in his head, and he fell to the ground with a thud.

I was too terrified to scream. I turned and ran when I saw my stalker pull the knife from Benny's neck and come running toward me. I wasn't fast enough, though; he tackled me to the ground and put duct tape over my mouth before he dragged me to the other side of the dumpster where nobody would see us if they left the club.

He sat on my chest and twirled the bloody knife around with a wicked smile. "Shh, pet. We're gonna have some fun."

I tried to scream from behind the tape, but it was just muffled. Stalker took the tip of the knife and ran it down my cheek and through the skin with a dark laugh. I screamed in pain, but he kept on. Cut, cut, cut, numerous times on each cheek, from the bottom of my eye socket to my chin. Then he started in on my neck. My salty tears streamed down my face and stung the open wounds with a burning pain. He began making slices on my neck next.

"Since you think you're too fucking good to be with me, then I'll make sure nobody else gets to have you, either, bitch," he said with a terrifying, murderous grin. "Then, I'll take you back to my place where you'll be my little pet. You'll be so ugly nobody will want you. But I'll still want you. And if you try to run away, I'll start cutting your body too. In fact, I might just take this knife"—he lifted it in front of me, blood dripping down the blade, and twirled it slowly—"and stick it right up your pussy. No man's gonna want your mangled, ugly cunt. But I will. I'll still love every part of you. But nobody else will. Just me."

I was growing weak from the blood loss and had stopped screaming. I couldn't buck him off, and I started to pray for death. I would rather die than be taken back to this maniac's house of horrors and live as a slave. I felt him poke the blade hard into the side of my neck and start to slice.

"Shit," he said.

I blinked open weak eyelids to see him staring down at my throat. "Shit!" Blood was arcing out so far, I could see it from the corner of my eye. "Nicked the damn jugular. Fuck!" He tried to cover it with his hand, so I closed my eyes and let my body go completely limp. "Dammit! Devon, baby, no!" He jumped off my body, and I cracked open an eye to see him run off. I tried to get up, but I passed out.

When I woke, I was in a strange house, lying on a soft bed. The open curtains on the window revealed the night sky. I sat up, panicked because I didn't know where I was.

"Oh good, you're awake."

I whipped my head around to see a strange man in a dress shirt, tie, and slacks looking at me. "Who are you?"

"I'm Alec. You're Devon, correct?"

I nodded. "What's going on? Where am I?"

"This is my home. I know you're scared but you needn't be. I found you behind that strip club. I followed the strong scent of blood and there you were. Another very large man was also there, but he was dead. You, however, were still alive, barely within an inch of your life, as a matter of fact. I put you in my car and brought you back here, where, unfortunately, I had to turn you to save you."

Oh, my God. The stalker. The stabbing. I lifted my hand to my face and felt long, ropey lines. I replayed what Alec just said. "What do you mean, turn me?"

"Vampire, darling." He put his hands behind his back and calmly paced. "And I'm so very sorry. The turning process wasn't quick enough to heal your wounds completely. By the third day, once the transformation was complete, they had already begun to heal and scab over. Even my saliva didn't help as I thought it would."

"Vampires, saliva, three days... what?" I put both hands to each side of my head and shook it back and forth. "You're crazy. I must be dreaming..."

"No, darling, you are not."

I stared at the man. He seemed polite and harmless, but definitely crazy. I suddenly felt sick. I got up and ran into the bathroom, barely making it to the toilet where my vomit was blood red and chunky. Alarmed, I gasped and then grabbed a nearby *towel to wipe my mouth. I turned on the faucet and cupped water into my hand to rinse my mouth out. I lifted my head to look in the mirror and screamed. "No!"*

18

TEAM EFFORT

Face

"I don't know what to do. It was a complete dead end," I said, pacing the floor of the clubhouse.

Viper, Shadow, Phoenix, and Andy stood around and listened to me rant. The alarm chirped and we turned around to see Venom walking in.

"What's up, Papa?" Shadow said with a grin.

"How's fatherhood?" Phoenix asked.

"Exhausting," he replied. "But amazing." He looked at me. "What's going on? I came as soon as I got the text."

I shook his hand. "I appreciate it, man. But you didn't have to. I know you have a lot going on."

"No, I wanted to. You all were there to help me protect Kalissa, and I want to help you find this girl. Your girl."

I shook my head. "She's not my girl, but we have to help her."

"He's totally in love with her," Jemini sing-songed as she exited the breakroom and headed toward the walkway that led to Cobalt.

I ignored her and held out Devon's phone. "I traced her cell to her address, but it was outside the building, along with some vampire blood I assume is hers," I said, filling Venom in. "But like I just told the guys, it's a dead end. I have no idea where they would take her. Or if she's even still alive."

"Not cool. Who is this girl, anyway? Where did you meet her?"

Venom asked.

Viper filled him in briefly.

"You two got a thing, though? The text said, 'Face's girl'." He smirked.

"Look, we were sorta starting to think about pursuing something, I guess you could say. She's as nerdy as I am, so it was slow moving. I don't have decades of experience with women like you guys."

They chuckled.

"It doesn't matter how much experience you have. Once you find the one, it's a wrap. You just know," Viper said.

"Hold on, I just thought of something," Shadow said. "Didn't you say Jemini contacted her on a burner phone at first before she gave you her real cell number?"

My eyes widened. "Craig, you big oaf. You're a genius. She told me she doesn't keep those very long but there were no phones at all in her apartment when I searched. I bet she still has it on her."

"I thought you couldn't trace those prepaid phones," Viper said.

"Most people can't. I have a few things I can try." I was just about to thank the guys and head to my office when MyAnna popped out of the walkway. "Face, there's a guy here asking for you. Says it's urgent." She looked at Viper. "He said Face or you, so you should both come."

We rushed into the Cobalt Room and MyAnna introduced us to a proper-looking vampire. "This is Gregory."

"What can we do for you?" Viper asked, hands on his hips.

"Which one of you is Mr. Face?" he asked, then eyed our cuts. "Oh, how silly of me. It's printed right there on your vest." He looked at me and asked, "Do you know Rocky? Young lady, computer expert, scars?" He pointed to his face.

I nodded, my normally slow heartrate increasing. "Yes, what about her?"

"She asked me to deliver a message." He pulled his cell phone from his pocket and then cleared his throat before adjusting his tie. I wanted to slap him and tell him to get on with it. He moved and spoke very slowly and Southern. I could tell he was a very old vampire. He read from the device. "Gregory, this is Rocky. I hate to ask but I need a favor. I've been taken by some men, and they took my other phone that had all my contacts in it. I need you to go to the Cobalt Room, it's a bar near the Quarter, and ask for Face or Viper. Tell them I've been kidnapped and I'm on a boat or yacht somewhere. I have no idea where, though. Please reply if you get this, and don't call this number, text only. Thanks."

"Oh, thank fuck she's still alive," I said on a relieved sigh.

Gregory made a face at my profanity and then cleared his throat. "Why would someone kidnap that nice girl?"

"How do you know her?" I asked.

"She tracked down my wife for me. I thought she died after I was turned, but it seems she's been living in Minneapolis, running a bakery. As a matter of fact, I was on my way to the airport to surprise her when I got this text message. I had my driver make a pitstop here first."

I put my hand out and he shook it. "Well, I thank you for taking the time. This really helps us."

"I just don't understand why someone would want to harm her."

"It's a long story, but we'll find her. Hey, can I have your phone for a second?" I asked.

"Sure," he said, handing it to me. I found the text from "Rocky" and didn't bother reading it, but instead quickly replied to it: *This is Parker, Gregory delivered your message. Here's my number, text me when you get this so we can come get you. Hang in there, beautiful.*

Then, I texted myself Devon's burner phone number, in case it was different from the one I already had, and also so I'd have Gregory's number. I handed him back the phone. "I sent her my number so she doesn't have to keep going through you. I also texted myself so now you have mine. Please hit me up if she makes contact again. Time is of the essence here."

He held up the phone and said, "Will do." He went to leave the club but turned around. "Oh, and Mr. Face? Rocky also asked me to tell you that she loves you."

I felt like I'd been punched in the stomach. I nodded and said my thanks before rushing back to my office to be alone.

Hours passed and no word from her. I kept my phone charged and face-up on my desk. I was starting to get sleepy and knew I wouldn't be able to stay up very much longer. I envied my older vampire brothers who could resist the sun's pull and needed less sleep.

Every hack I tried to trace the number with didn't work. Viper was right, these things were untraceable, and with someone like Devon, I was sure she had probably put extra protection on it to ensure that.

Unable to stay awake much longer, I dozed off with my head on my desk.

"Well, good morning. Or evening, I should say."

I looked over to see Martin sitting on the other side of the bed with his legs crossed, his arms hanging loosely on his lap.

"Martin? I asked groggily. "Did I fall asleep?" I shook my head, trying to remember how I got here.

"Yes, three days ago."

"What!" I sat upright, and as soon as I did, I immediately turned my head and vomited into a waiting pail set on the floor next to the bed. The solid red liquid confused me. "What the hell is going on?"

"I gave you a gift," he said, standing to come around the bed. "You remember that elixir I gave you? You're now a vampire, kid. Young and beautiful forever." He smiled as he clapped his hands in delight.

Wiping my mouth, I stared at him incredulously. "Vampire?

You've watched too many movies. I'm gonna go." I stood.

He stepped in front of me and made a tsking noise. "No, sirree, you are not leaving. I have to teach you how to be a vampire, so you'll need to stay another week here. In fact, if you wanted to move in, I have plenty of space. You can choose which bedroom you'd like."

This guy was sounding crazier by the second. "No, I'm good. I don't need to learn how to be a vampire. I'll Google it."

He threw back his head and laughed. "Oh, that wouldn't be wise. There's so much lore out there that you'll never find the right one. Tell me, what do you think happens if we go into the sun?"

"We sparkle?" *I deadpanned.*

He made a face. "Absolutely not. We die, Parker. Catch on fire as if someone has doused us in gasoline and lit a match."

I put my hand on my hip. This guy had to be messing with me, so I was going to mess with him right back. "Wait. No sun? But I can still use the tanning bed, right? Gotta maintain this golden glow." *I indicated my body.*

"You're not taking this seriously," *Martin huffed, frustrated.* "And absolutely not on the tanning bed. Those are nothing but UV rays. Instant death."

"Well, I'm hungry. Are there any of those little sausages left from the party last night?"

"Boy, have you been listening? That was three days ago!"

I looked down at my designer watch. He wasn't lying, the party had been on the twelfth and it was now the fifteenth of the month. "What the hell did you to me, Martin?" *I snapped.*

"And no sausages. Those were for the human guests. You can only consume blood and clear liquids like liquor or water."

I shook my head. "I'm leaving." *I barged past him and went to the front door. It was locked, and it appeared I needed a code to unlock it. I could feel Martin's presence behind me, and it occurred to me that I was able to hear him coming when he had approached so silently otherwise. I whirled around.* "Let me out. This is kidnapping."

He held out his cell phone to me. "Go ahead and call LAPD. I'm sure once they get here and you smell their delicious human blood, you'll have great restraint not to murder them violently as soon as they walk through the door."

I looked at him in horror. "You're serious about this, aren't you?"

He simply nodded as he repocketed his phone.

"Why would you do this to me?" *I screamed.* "Why?" *I rushed over to him with the intent of strangling him, shocked that I'd crossed the room in less than half a second. I stopped short, right in front of him.* "What was that?"

"We can move very fast. Much like your sparkly vampire you referenced earlier. That was about the only accurate part of that movie," *he added dryly.*

"This cannot be real," *I murmured, scrubbing a hand down my face.*

Martin approached me slowly and then looped his arm through mine. "Come, let's have a meal and talk."

I awoke from the dream, instantly irritated. I was so sick of dreaming about my past. I just wanted to forget how I became a monster, but my subconscious didn't think it was a good idea.

19

DAMSEL IN DISTRESS

Devon

A half-moon reflected off the water as the boat bobbed in place. There was no land to be seen in either direction, and I whimpered a little at the predicament I found myself in. I was tied to a chair on the deck of a massive yacht that looked like it cost hundreds of thousands of dollars.

The thugs had dragged me out of my room about an hour ago once the sun went down. I had awoken to a text from Parker and was so relieved Gregory had done as I'd asked. I replied and told him the situation, which wasn't much more than I had told Gregory. I didn't know anything—where we were, who my captors were. I suspected it was the human traffickers, but who knew at this point. All I knew was that nobody had a reason to kidnap me but them. I had quickly stowed the phone under the mattress when I heard footsteps pounding down the stairs. My hands were still bound in rope that was impossible to break, even with my enhanced strength.

Finally, two of them walked out onto the deck. They both wore jeans, T-shirts, and those ugly white tragedy theater masks with hoodies over their heads.

In a muffled voice from the plastic, the taller of the two said, "Rocky. We're going to keep you here until you tell us how you took our site down."

I looked into his brown eyes and said, "I already told you clowns. I did not take your site down! I don't have the power or knowledge to take down a huge site like that. Why would I do that, anyway? I just lost a big chunk of my income. Why would I shoot off my own foot like that?"

He came over and knocked my hood off my head. He grabbed my face and turned it side to side, "What the hell happened to your face?"

"A fucking monster like you. Don't touch me." I yanked my head back to loosen his grasp.

He looked at the shorter one, who said, "We think you discovered what we do on that site and your mortal coil came unraveled. You seem like the type of vampire who thinks she's still human and actually cares about those mouth-breathing blood bags."

I gritted my teeth. "While I do find what you do on that site vile fucking filth, I most certainly know I'm a vampire. And no, I don't care about humans in general," I lied. "But selling innocent children? You guys are sick fucks. Still, I did not take the site down. Maybe the cops did. Did you ever think about that?" I suggested, trying to get the heat off me.

"Yeah, we have. Because you tipped them off."

I craned my head back and stared at the starry night sky with a sigh. "Again, why do you think I would do that? Someone probably accidentally stumbled onto it and called the authorities. I knew it would happen eventually. Why not just make a new site?"

"Our programmer was killed last month. We're screwed without him."

I groaned. "Just freakin' let me go. Please. I can't help you."

The taller one chuckled beneath his mask and I noticed he had a long blond ponytail. "Oh, but you can. And you will. You're going to build us a new site, then we'll let you go. We'll pay you nicely to maintain it, too. But if it gets shut down again, we'll kill you."

The hell if I was gonna build them another one of those disgusting sites. However… were they actually going to give me access to the internet? "What, on this boat? You have computers and internet access here?"

"No, we're heading someplace that does. You'll stay until you get a new site up. Then you can go back to your shitty apartment in that shitty-ass city."

I pursed my lips and stared at the duo. "Take your masks off."

They laughed. "No," the taller one said.

"It's going to take me weeks or months to build a site like that," I lied. I had no idea how to build anything but a simple, basic website, but they didn't know that. "You're gonna wear those things the whole time?"

The shorter one nodded. "Yes."

"What are your names?" I asked.

"None of your fucking business, bitch."

"You guys sound like a dream to work for," I murmured. "Fine. I'll do it. But you could have just asked me instead of all these theatrics."

"No, because if you're the one who called the cops and reported our website, you would have turned us in."

I rolled my eyes. "Whatever." I huffed and stared at the duo. "Where are we headed, anyway?"

They looked at each other and said nothing.

"What? Who am I gonna tell? I'm out here in the middle of nowhere and you took my effing phone."

"Virgin Islands," the shorter one answered.

Ponytail smacked him upside the head with a scoffing noise. "Stupid."

I was relieved I knew where we were headed. "Now, can I get some blood, please? I'm hungry."

The shorter one untied me from the chair and manhandled me by the arm to below deck, where he stopped and pulled a blood bag from a fishing cooler. He pressed it up against my chest, where I held onto it with my tied hands before he threw me into my room and locked the door.

I yanked the phone from under the mattress and checked it. No more texts, but that wasn't surprising. I was lucky to have received a reply from Parker due to our remote location. I sent him one last text: *We're headed for the Virgin Islands. I gotta power this down to save battery. I'll make contact when I get there. As suspected, it's the human traffickers. These goons are going to try to force me to build them a new website so I'll have internet access. Update later xo <3*

I begrudgingly powered down the phone and ripped open the blood bag. As I was drinking it, I thought about the dream I'd had today. I hadn't dreamt of my past in a very long time. I loathed thinking about the worst day of my existence. Alec saved my life, but he also ended it. I hated him for a long time, but now that I'd been a vampire for so long, I realized he had the best intentions and wasn't trying to hurt me or ruin my life. I just couldn't believe I'd have to look like this forever. There was not going to come a time where I'd get old and wrinkled and maybe the scars wouldn't be noticeable.

After two years with Alec and his clan, I left him and went to live alone in Alabama. I was still technically a missing person. I left my family, friends, and job behind and after creating a false identity, I took night classes in computer science. I basically self-taught the rest of what I'd learned—and I was still learning. In the nineties, technology was still very new that I had to keep up or be left out. I learned quickly that me getting a regular job was out of the question. I couldn't deal with the stares and questions. No matter how friendly I was to people, they still looked afraid of me. Especially little kids who had no filter and would point and sometimes cry.

I had watched a lot of tutorials online on how to apply "full coverage" makeup, and while it did actually help me to look less hideous if I took the time to do all the highlighting and contouring that came with it, I mostly found it a waste of time. It was easier to just hide behind my hair and this hood.

After finishing my blood bag, I lay on the bed and stared at the ceiling. I wished they'd untie my hands. What was I going to do against two strong male vampires? It wasn't like I could escape either. I was so used to being on the computer that I was going to go stir crazy in here without so much as a book to read. I got up and tried the door. I used vampire strength to try to break the lock, but it wouldn't budge. They must have done something to it.

Sighing, I went back to the bed and closed my eyes, praying to whoever would listen that Parker would find me before these thugs found out I couldn't do what I said I would and build them a super secure website on the Dark Web. Those website addresses weren't like normal ones, they were scrambled and complicated.

I hated feeling like the damsel in distress waiting to be rescued, but I literally had no other way out of this unless Parker found me. The most depressing part about it was—if I'd never met Parker, I wouldn't have had anyone to call to try and save me. I'd have been good and truly fucked.

20

WAITING GAME
Face

I paced the breakroom, furious. "I'm going to kill them," I snarled after reading Devon's latest text.

"I'll hold them down for you," Phoenix replied from the table where he and Jemini sat. "Sick assholes trafficking kids and now kidnapping Devon. I say we make it nice and slow."

I chewed my thumbnail. "I agree."

"You should cut their dicks off first," Jemini said. "Just in principle for being perverts."

Cringing at the thought, I simply nodded. "I'll let you do that part."

She grinned. "Happily."

"You are *not* going, so you won't be doing that," Phoenix said to Jemini.

"I know," she replied with a pout. "A girl can dream."

"You gotta stay here and hold down the technology portion of this fort," I replied, still pacing.

Phoenix patted the chair next to him. "Sit down. It'll calm you."

I stared at the chair and reluctantly obeyed. "Once she reaches the Virgin Islands and gets online, I'll be able to easily track her location. This waiting game is fucking killing me."

"I know," Jemini said. "I've never seen you so wound up."

Venom walked in and opened the refrigerator. He pulled out

food to make a sandwich. "What are you guys talking about in here?"

"Just trying to plan for when we hear from Devon."

"Yeah?" Venom replied, rifling through the drawer for a knife. "What's the plan?"

"We kill them," I said through gritted teeth.

The wolf chuckled. "I mean, before that."

"Hop on a plane, swoop in, save the girl, kill the bad guys," Phoenix replied.

"You make it sound so easy," Venom replied, pushing the bread together on his sandwich and lifting it to his face. "Life isn't an action movie."

"How's baby?" Jemini asked. "I want to meet him so bad!"

He swallowed his bite and smiled. "He's perfect. Kalissa's an amazing mom. I offered to hire a nanny to come in during the day to help, but she refused. She's stubborn like that." He grinned and shook his head. "She's exclusively breastfeeding and said she's fine."

"Is she able to keep her weight up and all that? I know you have to, like, double your calorie intake when you're nursing," Jemini said. "I hope that doesn't sound insensitive."

Venom shook his head. "No, not at all. I appreciate the concern, actually. She's doing great. I've become quite the cook and make her finish her food. She looks so much healthier now with some curves and a little bit to grab onto." He winked.

Gag.

"That's great, I'm so happy for you. Auntie Jemini is ready for a visit when she's up to it." She rubbed her hands together.

He laughed again. "Soon, girl."

I set my phone on the table, face-up, and stared at it.

"Okay, we need to get your mind off of this," Jemini said. "Tell me a story."

"Ooh, I wanna hear a story," Bloome said as she wandered in with Shadow trailing behind her.

I looked up at them. "What kind of story? I'm a computer geek, not a novelist."

"Why don't you tell them how you met us?" Shadow said. "I remember the day like it was yesterday."

"Me too," Venom said around a mouthful.

I looked at the girls. "Fine."

"What are we talking about in here?" MyAnna asked, walking in. She began tidying up and cleaning. I remember her complaining but I secretly thought she liked being the mama boss around here.

"Face is gonna tell us how he got into the Nighthawks."

"Ooh!" MyAnna said. "Yes, please!"

I chuckled and shook my head. "Well, you guys know I used to model, right? Of course you do," I said, glaring at Shadow who had a mischievous glint in his eye since he was the one who'd put my underwear ad up in the breakroom. "Well, the guy who turned me was a movie producer. He tricked me into being turned, actually. Told me the vial of vampire blood was some immortality elixir. It was just his blood mixed with mine. I was so stupid and naïve." I blew out a breath.

"You were only twenty-one. Nobody's very smart at that age," Bloome said, her hands folded on the table.

"I know, but still. I wanted fame so badly, I just wasn't thinking. Well, this man, this movie producer, I believe he thought he had a shot at me. Turned me and then spent two years guilting me into staying. Saying I owed him, and that we would make a great team. He made passes at me, but I just wasn't the one for him. I truly only think he wanted me because of my looks." I winced inside. I hated even bringing up my appearance. "I told him several times that I was straight, but he thought he could convince me otherwise or something… I don't know. Anyway, one day I just left. Packed my shit while he was on the set and took a car down to the nearest Greyhound station. The bus to New Orleans was the next one leaving, so I bought a ticket and disappeared from Southern California."

"That sounds like Vane's story. Very similar," MyAnna commented.

I smiled at her. "It is. He did the same thing after being turned. California is no place for vampires. *The Lost Boys* be damned."

They all chuckled.

"I enrolled in online classes for computer science with a minor in engineering and worked an online job doing IT repair remotely while I finished schooling. I got my degree in three years and landed a sweet job with the biggest tech company in the area. I told them I could only work at night for personal reasons, and they let me work remotely.

"One night about a year ago, I saw a listing on the supernatural job listings site, and—"

Andy—Eagle—wandered into the breakroom. "What's a supernatural job listings site? That's seriously a thing?"

I looked up at him to see amusement dancing in his light-blue eyes. "Yes, it's for supes who only hire other supes."

"Interesting. So, I have a question. How are you that tan?" Eagle asked, pointing at my arms.

"Spray tans," I murmured.

"Why?" he asked, folding his arms across his cut.

I blew out a breath. "Because I like them, okay? I fit in better with humans when I look like them." I looked at Jemini and Phoenix. "Anyway, Vane had put in a listing for an IT guy. We met at the Devil's Den for a quick interview, and I was patched and tatted the next week. The rest, as they say, is history."

Viper came into the breakroom. "True story."

Smiling at him. "Vane saved my ass. I was severely depressed at my new existence, and he showed me I could live a mostly normal life despite all the negatives that came with vampirism. That we could do good in the world, in spite of our sunlight problem. I have not regretted one day being a part of this Nighthawks family. Not once."

MyAnna wiped a tear. "That was amazing. Thank you for sharing with us."

Viper kissed the top of her head and squeezed her to him. "Face has been a godsend. We've saved so many people thanks to his knowledge of computers. Us old geezers have no idea how to navigate that shit."

"Speak for yourself, Gramps. I ain't no geezer," Shadow quipped, chuckling.

"No, you're not," Bloome replied, leaning over to kiss him on the mouth.

Damn, I missed Devon so much. My stomach lurched again at the thought of her in any sort of danger or being hurt.

"Looks like y'all saved each other," Jemini added.

"It's true," Viper said. "We wouldn't be the strong club we are now without that big brain of his. We were a force to be reckoned with before. But now? We're un-fucking-stoppable."

Nods and sounds of agreement came from the group.

Just then, my phone chimed with a text. I snatched it up and read the message.

Devon: *We're in Charlotte Amalie. Orange mansion, number 23 on the gate.*

I stood, the chair squeaking behind me. I read the group the text message.

"Let's go. I've got a plane waiting at the airport," Viper said, pulling his phone from his pocket. "I'm texting the pilot now to meet us there."

We quickly ditched the cuts and jeans and changed into all-black tactical gear we rarely used. I felt empowered in the cargo pants, zip jacket, a balaclava, and boots. We were also armed to the teeth with pistols, pepper balls, and mini grenades.

The ride to the airport was nerve-wracking. I had no idea what to expect. A quick check of my phone showed it was one a.m.

Since we rarely ever left New Orleans, Viper had to pay a pretty penny to charter a plane. Phoenix parked the van at the edge of the tarmac. We sprinted to the waiting aircraft and hopped inside.

"Charlotte Amalie, Jerry," Viper said to the pilot.

"You got it," Jerry replied, and we were up and off.

I stared out the window, chewing on my thumbnail. I felt a hand on my shoulder. I looked up to see Harlan giving me a fatherly look. "It's okay. We're going to get your girl. Those assholes are no match for us."

I nodded and blew out a breath. "I know. Thank you for coming. I know you have a lot going on."

He grinned. "Ride or die, brother."

21

CHARLOTTE AMALIE
Devon

I woke on the second night to realize that the yacht had stopped moving. I got out of bed, removed the cell phone from its hiding spot, and shoved it into my bra. In the adjoining bathroom, I gave my teeth a finger scrub. Just then, the door to my room opened.

"Let's go, Frankenstein. Time to get to work."

"Don't call me that," I snapped as the goon, still wearing that stupid mask, grabbed me by the arm and hustled me up the stairs and across the deck.

He gripped me tight as I took the steps down off the ship. I was then thrown into a black sedan with blacked-out windows. I paid careful attention to the street signs. Charlotte Amalie was the city we were in. That was good. Even though the thugs were both sitting up in the front seats, I couldn't risk pulling out the phone and texting Parker. Not yet.

The ride was short. We pulled up at a large mansion, painted a dull orange, with the numbers *23* on the outside of the big black gate we'd just driven through. I was again forced out of the car by my arm. "I can walk just fine. You don't need to manhandle me like a damn prisoner."

"Shut up," the goon said as he walked me up the steps of the place.

How much money did these guys have? They were paying me a thousand a month to maintain the malware situation. I was thinking

I should have charged them double—especially if they were this loaded.

It's all dirty money.

I was plunked onto a plush white couch in the living room. "Stay there. Don't move or I'll cut your lips off," Ponytail said to me.

"Rude," I said as they walked away.

Once I was alone, I looked around the room. I couldn't see any cameras but that didn't mean they weren't here. After making sure they weren't coming back, I went to every knick-knack and statue to make sure there were no hidden cameras. I quickly withdrew my phone and texted Parker my location. With relief I wasn't caught, I shoved it back into my bra just as I heard footsteps coming around the corner.

"Stand up, let's go," Ponytail said. I was relieved he didn't grab my arm and was going to let me walk on my own.

"Where are we going?" I asked, looking around to familiarize myself with the place.

"Shut up and stop asking questions. You're on my nerves already, Frankenstein."

"Don't you get hot under that mask? Oops, that was a question. I mean, you should take that mask off, it's gotta be hot under there."

With vampire speed, he backhanded me, and I fell to the floor. I put my hands to my face and scowled up at him. "Asshole."

"Shut your fucking pie hole. I won't tell you again, bitch."

I stood and followed him down a hallway. He led me to a room that had a bed, dresser, computer station, and an adjoining bathroom. After pushing me inside, I almost lost my balance and fell again. The stinging on my cheek persisted but would be gone soon, thanks to the quick healing. "Stay in here and shut up. Get started on building that website." He pointed to the computer.

As he was about to close the door, I said, "Wait. Can't you

please untie my hands? I can't work like this."

I saw his brown eyes move down toward my hands. With a huff, he pulled out a pocketknife and sliced through them.

"Thank you," I said, rubbing my red, raw skin.

He slammed the door in my face and locked it from the outside.

I searched the room for cameras and only saw a webcam on the computer. I quickly pulled out the phone and powered it on. I had a quarter battery power left. I shot off another text to Parker: *I'm inside this mansion, they have me in a back room. There's a computer here so I'll try to make contact that way.*

I went to shove the phone under the mattress, and it buzzed before I could power it down.

Parker: *We're on our way. Hang tight, beautiful.*

Tears welled up in my eyes. I couldn't believe he cared that much for me. He said *we*, so I assumed he was bringing a couple of guys with him. *Smart.* I powered down the phone, went over to the computer, and sat in the chair. After booting it up, I quickly checked the internet access and smiled when I saw WiFi. I went to the settings and wrote down the IP address with a pencil and pad of paper I found in the top desk drawer.

A message box popped up on the screen: *We're watching everything you do, Frank. You do anything but build that website, we'll see every keystroke and site you visit. There's a credit card in the drawer if you need to buy software. No funny business. We'll be monitoring purchases as well.*

I laughed. I could clone this computer faster than they could blink and then do anything I wanted, and they'd see nothing. They were lucky there was no reply option because I had a few middle-finger emojis I'd love to send back. I ripped off a scrap of paper, licked it, and stuck it to the webcam in case they wanted to watch me through it. "Screw you." I flipped off the camera.

I pulled out the phone and texted Parker the IP address, thought maybe it could help him find me faster. After powering it down again, I put it under the mattress and went to work.

22

SEARCH & RESCUE

Face

We landed at the small airport at three a.m., and quickly deplaned. Jerry was ordered to stay put. An unmarked shuttle van awaited us, and after we all piled in, the driver asked us where to.

I looked down at the text I'd gotten from Devon right before we landed. It had been too easy to track her exact location from my tablet using the IP address. "Twenty-three Crown Mountain Road. But... you can drop us nearby and we'll walk the rest of the way. It's a, uh, surprise visit."

He eyed our tactical clothing and said in broken English, "Uh, sure. That not too far from here, be about ten minutes."

We rode in silence. My stomach was a ball of nerves. Every lieutenant but Andy had come, and I was overwhelmed with gratitude. They didn't have to risk their lives for me—for Devon. But they were. We had no idea how many men or vampires were in the house.

After a few minutes, the driver stopped the van on the side of the road and said, "It's up the hill, about three houses. Can't miss it."

"Thanks," Viper said, handing the man cash. "Stay here and wait, we'll be out in less than an hour. Kill the lights, please."

"You got it, boss man," he replied, turning the engine off.

The five of us huddled up in front of the van. "Did she say where in the house she was?" Viper asked me.

"She just said a back bedroom."

"I say the two of you go in, the three of us will surround the house, front and back," Shadow said.

"I agree," Phoenix said. "You guys locked and loaded?"

Rolling my eyes, I held up my pistol. "Yes, Rambo."

Viper pulled his balaclava up over his face. We did the same as we ran up the street. Hiding behind a large palm bush at the front of the property, we ducked down.

"I forgot there was a gate. Craig, go break the lock," Viper instructed.

"No," I said, putting a hand on Shadow's arm. "They probably have an alarm inside that triggers when the gate is opened. Probably have cameras, too. I say we go around the back, jump over the fence."

"Okay," Viper said. "Let's go."

We used vampire speed to get to the back of the house. The same black wrought-iron fencing surrounded the whole property. The one at the back had pointed tips on each bar. In the backyard was a large swimming pool with string lights up on the back porch littered with patio furniture.

"Hey, look," Venom said. "There's a gate." He asked me, "Think it'll set off any alarms?"

I went over to it and shook my head. "No, there's nothing electrical here. So unless they have an invisible fence, we should be able to break it and sneak in undetected."

Shadow twisted the padlock off and dropped it to the ground.

As silent as ghosts, we crept into the backyard and spread out. "Look in the windows, discreetly," Viper said into our earpieces.

All the lights were on in the house. The curtains were open, and we could see three individuals in the living room watching television. There was one other in the kitchen using the microwave. All males.

I went around to the side of the house and saw three sets of windows. Unfortunately, they all had blackout shutters on them. I tapped lightly on the first one and then put my back up against the wall, out of sight. Nobody responded. Onto the next, I did the same with no response. If she wasn't in this third room, I would have to assume they had moved her, or she was elsewhere in the house. I tapped on the window lightly with my pistol and hid. With my sensitive hearing, I heard somebody stir. My heart raced. The shutters moved and I saw Devon's face peer out. I jumped in front of the window, and she looked like she was about to scream until I lowered my face covering.

"It's me," I said quietly. "Open the window!"

She shook her head. "I already tried. It doesn't open."

"Hang tight," I said, putting a finger up. I pressed the com button on my earpiece. "Face to Nighthawks, I found her. Back bedroom. I'm gonna have to break the window. Be prepared for chaos."

"Copy," they replied.

"Shadow, go find Face and help. Venom, Phoenix, get out of the yard but wait behind the fence. Just watch for anything."

"Roger," they replied.

Shadow materialized next to me, and I jumped. He hadn't done that in a while. In fact, we should have just sent him in there to begin with. This was less risky, I supposed.

"Grab whatever you need and get back. I'm breaking the window."

Devon yanked the plastic shutters off the window and then pulled something out from under the mattress.

"Ready?" I asked Craig.

He nodded.

I used my gun to break the window. "Come on!" I said to Devon, looking around. She jumped out the window and into my arms.

"Thank you," she sobbed into my shoulder.

I had so many feelings going at once. Relief but still fear. We weren't close to being out of the woods yet.

"Let's get you out of here, beautiful." We ducked low and ran toward the gate. We froze when we heard a gunshot.

"Shit," Shadow said. "Stay here." He disappeared but we didn't stay put. We rounded the corner into the main part of the yard and saw Viper on the ground, bleeding from his shoulder. He was conscious and looked murderous.

"Breaking the window must have tripped a silent alarm," Devon whispered.

"You're probably right," I said, grabbing her hand and yanking her to the side of the house, where I told her to stay. I went around slowly and watched Shadow appear in front of one of the guys and break his neck, then shoot him in the head. He popped off two more shots and hit the other two in the head. They crumbled to ash, their clothing the only thing left.

"Come on!" I pulled Devon around the corner and headed for the gate. The last one spotted us and aimed his pistol at us. "Where do you think you're going, Frank? We're gonna find you, you ugly-ass bitch!" He shot off a round right at us.

I pushed her to the ground, lifted my gun, and aimed it straight for center mass. The bullet hit him in the chest, and he went down with a thud. "Shut the fuck up, asshole."

"Dude! You hit him from like thirty yards away!" Venom called from behind the gate.

"Nobody fucks with my woman," I snapped. With my adrenaline flowing, I pulled her to stand, pushed her hood back, and grabbed her face. My lips crashed down onto hers, and she wrapped her arms around my neck and kissed me back.

Phoenix whistled from behind the gate. "Later, lovebirds, let's roll."

Shadow picked up Viper and used vampire speed to rush him out of the yard. We all followed.

We ran down the street, and the driver started the van as soon as he saw us rushing toward him.

"Back to the airport," Shadow said, setting Viper into the first bench seat.

"Is he bleeding?" the driver asked as he pealed off onto the road.

"It'll heal," Viper said through gritted teeth, rolling his shoulder. "It's a through and through."

Devon and I sat on the third-row bench. I squeezed her hand. "Are you okay? Did they hurt you?"

She shook her head and looked at me with big, shiny green eyes. "Thank you for saving me." She looked around the van. "All of you. I didn't deserve it, but I'm in your debt."

"I'd call it a win for everyone. Four human-trafficking pieces of shit are dead, and that website is gone."

"There are lots of others," Devon said quietly.

"Then with your help, we'll take those down, too," Shadow said, turning around and looking at us.

She smiled. "Of course."

The van went silent, and I looked at Devon. "Frank?"

She rolled her eyes. "Frankenstein."

I set my jaw and growled, "I should have shot him twice."

I asked Phoenix to drop us off at Devon's apartment. She was going to get some things and then come stay at the clubhouse with me for a while.

"What the hell? Why is my door unlocked?" she asked as we reached her apartment.

"I don't know. When I came here looking for you, it was already unlocked so I left it that way."

We wandered inside, and she took off the hoodie and threw the burner phone onto the couch. "I wonder if they broke in here and were looking around before they found me on the street. Doesn't look like anything's missing."

"That makes sense." I looked at the lock. "Yeah, the lock's broken. I should have noticed that before."

"So, how did you know which apartment was mine?" she asked.

I grinned. "I broke into the office and found paperwork for an apartment leased to Devon Smith. I took a chance."

"You criminal, you," she replied, turning down the hallway toward the bedroom.

I grabbed her shoulder, spun her around, and pushed her up against the hallway wall. I bent down and sealed my lips over hers, kissing her in a way she'd know I wasn't letting her out of my sight. She wrapped her arms around my neck, and I reached under her shirt to unclasp her bra from the back one-handed. I broke the kiss and tore her shirt off over her head, then tossed her bra to the floor.

Panting, she unzipped my jacket and slid it off my arms where it landed with a thud. Then she urgently pulled my belt buckle loose, yanked it, and threw it to the floor like it was a snake about to attack her. Smiling, she unbuttoned my pants and ran the zipper down.

"I'm so fucking hard, I need to be inside you," I murmured as she stared into my eyes while she shoved my pants down.

She licked her lips with a grin as she pulled her jeans down and shimmied out of them after toeing off her boots. I quickly got rid of my boots and kicked out of my pants.

"Fuck, that's beautiful," she said, grabbing my painfully hard cock and stroking it. I shuddered. It had been way too long, and I wasn't going to last, I just knew it.

I got down on my knees, pushed her legs apart, and gripped her hips. I felt her hands go into my hair with a moan as I licked her slit and my tongue wiggled it inside, finding her swollen bud. I sucked on it and then pushed two fingers inside her. "Goddamn, you taste delicious," I murmured while I ate her pussy like a starving man.

Her legs began to tremble, and she was mewling and mumbling incoherent words. When her grip on my hair tightened, I felt her walls squeeze around my fingers as my tongue continued to lavish her. "Parker," she let out on a breathy moan. "Oh, God."

I stood, wiped my face, and then picked her up, wrapping her legs around my waist. I shoved my cock into her dripping wet hole and started pumping. I could feel her pussy still spasming from the orgasm and moved my hips faster. She grabbed my face and kissed me while we fucked hard and fast. I felt her walls squeeze around me again, and her nipples pebbled against my chest. A rush of tingles raced through my groin, and my balls seized up a split second before I exploded inside of her. She screamed and shuddered against me. "Oh, my God!"

"Holy shit," I grunted, still pumping into her slowly as I milked my climax.

She leaned her face into my shoulder as we stood there, not moving, her back against the wall, her breasts pressed to my chest. She lifted her head to look at me. "That was... I don't think I've ever come that hard."

I pressed my lips to hers once more. "Me neither." I looked into her face and brushed her hair away from her cheek. "I love you, Devon."

Her beautiful green eyes welled up. "I know. You risked your life to save me. If that's not love, I don't know what is." She stroked my cheek with her thumb. "I love you, too, Parker."

23

SEXY MONSTERS

Devon

As day approached, we fell asleep in my bed after our little hallway tryst. I was still trembling from the experience, and Parker had held me tight until we fell asleep. It was now just a little past three p.m. and I was wide awake. Parker was sleeping like the dead. I forgot how much sleep I needed when I was a new vampire. Propping myself up on my elbow I watched him sleep. He looked perfect and content. I brushed some hair off his forehead and traced my fingers down his face and over his perfect, smooth skin. I traced his jawline and then touched his lips with featherlight strokes.

We had fallen asleep nude and with just a sheet covering us. I pulled it down to expose his torso. I ran my fingers down his smooth chest, over the massive bird tattoo on his shoulder, and over the bumps and ridges of his washboard stomach. How did I manage to get this fine specimen to fall for me? I would never figure it out, but one thing I knew for sure… I had been waiting for him. I didn't think love would ever be in the cards for me—it was what I told myself when I was lonely. But somewhere deep down, my soul knew it wasn't complete. I felt empty, my heart permanently broken from all the shit I'd endured up until this point. Now, I could feel the shattered organ begin to knit together and beat strongly in my chest for this man.

Sliding the sheet lower, I gazed down at his beautiful cock. It was hard and ready to go. I stroked it softly like it was my favorite new pet, and I giggled when it twitched under my touch. Parker stirred in his sleep, and I was so aroused I couldn't wait for him to wake up. I threw the sheet off us, slid over, and straddled his waist, supporting myself on my knees. Grabbing his thick man meat, I impaled myself on it and groaned as I slid down. As I began to rock my hips, Parker blinked open his eyes. Then, they went wide.

"Good morning. Or afternoon," I said, licking my lips with a naughty grin and staring into his eyes. My hair framed my face and ran down my shoulders, covering my breasts. It swished along my body with my gyrations.

Parker grabbed my hips and matched my rhythm. "I can't think of a better way to wake up." He looked down at our connection. "Damn, you're so tight and wet, I may be a five-pump chump like earlier."

"Make me come," I whispered, still staring into his hungry blue eyes.

He reached up, grabbed one nipple, and began to roll it between his thumb and forefinger. With the other hand, he pinched my clit gently. A full-body shudder rocketed through my body. That delicious pressure in my channel began to build, my breathing increasing as a climax was building, threatening to erupt like a volcano.

Waves of tingles exploded where his finger spun in circles until I stopped rocking and threw my head back, my eyes closing. "Oh, my God, Parker."

"Look at me while you come," he commanded, pinching my nipple harder.

"Ohhhh…" I opened my eyes and stared deep into his before shuddering. "How do you make me come so fast?"

He grinned wickedly before lifting me off him. I landed on my back on the bed and then he grabbed my ankle and flipped me over onto my stomach. "Up on your knees, baby."

I obeyed, thrusting my ass toward him. He used two fingers to open my folds and then teased the entrance with his cock. "So beautiful. It's soaked and ready for me." He slid his dick inside and we both groaned.

As he slowly began to ride me, he grabbed a fistful of my hair and yanked my head back as he increased his jolting movements in and out of me.

"Yes, fuck me hard," I breathed, loving how he was controlling my body. "Beat up that pussy cat, handsome. Make me come all over your cock."

"Devon, that dirty talk isn't going to make me last any longer," he growled, his thrusts a punishing pace now, the smell of sex and the sounds of our bodies slapping overtaking the room. I reached down and fingered my clit, squeezing my walls around him each time he slammed inside me. A quick orgasm flooded me, right as Parker yanked my head to the side, bit down on my neck, and sucked hard. It launched me into orbit, my head becoming dizzy with pheromones and lust as another surprise climax crested, causing me to shudder hard and release a mewl that sounded foreign, even to me. I'd never had sex and been bitten before. It was indescribable.

After two long pulls of my blood, he slammed into me one last time and released all his cum inside me with an animalistic grunt. We collapsed in exhaustion.

I lay there in a stupefied post-coital coma, staring at the ceiling. Parker rolled over toward me and captured my lips in a long, drugging kiss that made a girly moan float from my mouth. With a grin, he wiped his bottom lip with his thumb and said, "Bathroom," as he got up and went around the bed to the restroom. I heard the faucet turn on, and then he came back with a warm washcloth. He wiped all the wet and dried slime from my thighs and then gently ran it up my slit. It felt so good. After washing himself off with it, he threw it back into the bathroom and came back to bed. He wrapped me in his arms, and I laid my head on him, my hair fanned out on his chest.

"You're my hero, you know," I said, drawing circles with my finger on his pec muscle.

He looked down at me. "I don't think I'm anyone's hero. Those assholes took you, and we got you back. I'm sure you'd have found a way out, hacked your way into the FBI's tip line or something," he said, chuckling.

"They were watching my every keystroke. It was going to take me days if not a couple weeks to clone the system so I could go to sites freely without them watching. The phone had one bar left on it and I had no charger."

Parker stared into my eyes and stroked his thumb on my cheek. "I don't know what I would have done if something happened to you. I was so angry and hurt when you didn't show up at the clubhouse, and then felt lower than scum when I found out you'd been taken. I have your phone, by the way, it was outside the building against the wall."

"Oh, good. I thought they still had it."

"No, it's charging in my room at the clubhouse."

I laid my head back onto his firm chest. "Parker, how come you never asked me how my face got like this?"

He was quiet for a few long seconds, stroking my arm in soft circles. "Because it doesn't matter to me. Honestly, I don't even see the scars. Plus, I figured if you wanted me to know, you'd tell me eventually. And if not, I would be okay with it, too. I can't imagine it would be anything you'd want to relive."

Tears welled up in my eyes and I nodded silently. "Thank you. It's still a little traumatic to talk about but I'll tell you about it later. I'm too happy right now to be brought down with those memories."

"It sounds like you've been through it, beautiful. And now being kidnapped by those sick fucks. I'm glad they're dead and I hope it doesn't leave you with any emotional scars. They didn't hurt you, did they?"

I looked up at him. "No, just manhandled me a bit. They thought I brought their site down and were going to lock me back up until I built them another one."

"You know how to build a site like that?" he asked.

I snorted. "No way. I mean, I can build a regular website but nothing that complex and protected. Nor would I want to. If I had figured it out, I would have just thrown it up on the D.W. and then exploded it as soon as they let me go. I'm glad they're dead."

"Are you okay, though, I mean, really? Traumatized from being snatched like that?" he asked. "I'm sure you were terrified."

"Well, I use sarcasm to hide my fear usually, so they didn't know I was afraid they'd kill me, but I really was terrified, Parker." I shuddered at the way they looked at me from behind those theater masks.

He kissed the top of my head. "You'll be okay. I won't let you out of my sight."

I shook my head a little. "I just don't know how I'm supposed to go back to normal after all of that."

"I didn't say you'd go back to normal, I said you'd be okay. And you will because you're leaving this place and moving in with me."

My finger paused at the circles I was drawing, and I craned my head to smile up at him. "You asking me to move in with you?"

His sexy lips turned up to form a sexy, lazy grin that turned my insides to mush. "I'm not asking. I'm telling you that's what you're doing. I'm not going to lose you again. You're my person. My other half. I know that now."

My heart fluttered and my belly flopped at his words. "Okay."

The sun was almost down so I said, "Let's shower and go to your clubhouse. I need to thank everyone personally."

He nodded. "Can I use your computer first? My phone's dead."

"Sure," I said, getting up and throwing his T-shirt on. It came down to my midthigh.

"God, you look sexy in my shirt," he said, sliding his boxers on.

I led him to the living room and booted up the machine. After putting my password in, I almost died of embarrassment. I put my hands over my eyes with a groan as Parker chuckled.

"I'm never ever going to be able to scrub that photo from the internet, am I?" he asked.

I pursed my lips to stop from laughing. "Came right up on a Google search. Sorry, been crushing on you and had to at least have you on one of my screens."

He pulled me flush to his body and gave me a long, luxurious kiss that made my toes curl. "Go hop in the shower, I'll be right there to scrub you down." He waggled his eyebrows at me before he sat in the chair and pulled up a search engine.

24

UNFINISHED BUSINESS

Face

I rolled my eyes as squeals erupted when Devon and I walked into the clubhouse carrying suitcases. Jemini, Bloome, MyAnna, and Kalissa were standing around talking. MyAnna was holding a bundle wrapped in a blue blanket, rocking the baby back and forth.

"I think you've met all the hens so far, right?" I asked Devon as we approached the group.

"Hens?" Kalissa asked. "I thought we were the old ladies."

Devon wrinkled her nose. "Old ladies?"

"It's a term for the women in committed relationships with the men in the club," MyAnna said. "I find the term crude as well, so we don't really use it around here."

I wrapped my arm around Devon's shoulders. "You wanna be my old lady?"

She grinned up at me. "Sure. You can call me whatever you want." She waggled her eyebrows at me.

"We're not hens," Jemini said, rolling her eyes.

"At least we don't have to take on some lame club nickname," Bloome said, and the girls laughed.

"What would I be called then?" Kalissa asked.

"Wolf Mama," Bloome said with a wink.

"I can't believe you let them call you Face," Devon said, her eyes sparkling with amusement.

I pulled her closer and bit back a grin. "Well, I wanted Dick C. Normus but the boss wouldn't sign off on it. You know, Dick for short."

The girls groaned and I chuckled.

"You're so bad," Devon said. She leaned up and whispered in my ear, "But that name would have been totally accurate."

MyAnna and Jemini made scoffing noises. "Gross," Jemini said, making a face.

Damn vampire hearing.

"I know you're not talking about your dick in front of my woman," Viper said, walking up and putting his good arm around MyAnna's shoulders.

"Of course not," I said cheekily. "How's the shoulder?" I pointed to it.

He rolled his shoulder in a circle. "Stiff but getting better every hour."

"You wanna hold him?" MyAnna asked Vane.

He made a face. "He's cute but I'll pass."

"My turn," Jemini said, rubbing her hands together and then out for the baby.

I got closer and looked down at the sleeping infant. He looked the same as he did in the photos, and his heart was beating so fast. He smelled good enough to eat and that was my cue to exit stage left. I didn't know how Jemini had such restraint.

"Cute kid. Congratulations," I said to Kalissa before grabbing Devon's hand and leading her up to my apartment.

"Keep it down once you get up there, the baby's sleeping!" Bloome called out, giggling.

Devon's eyes went wide. "Oh, my God. You guys can hear each other doing the nasty in here, can't you, with all these vampires around?"

I chuckled and pointed to my nightstand. "Top-of-the-line noise-canceling headphones."

"Better order me some, too," she murmured as she set her bag down and looked around. "Quaint, I like it."

I shrugged and hung my jacket up on the hook on the back of the door. "Thanks. I don't spend too much time up here, just sleeping and showering." I turned around and Devon was standing right in front of me.

She shoved me gently against the door. "Maybe you'll want to spend more time up here now that I'm here," she whispered against my lips.

Grabbing her hair at the back, I used it to tip her head back and stare into her eyes. "I think you're right." I kissed her long and slow, my cock already hard and ready for round three. After a few minutes, I pulled away and turned around to make sure the door was locked. Then, I pushed her onto the bed where she landed with a giggle.

She unzipped her hoodie and shimmied out of it. Her burner phone fell to the floor. "Shit, I better charge that. Hold that thought." She grinned at me before picking it up and rummaging through her bag for a charger. As soon as it was plugged in, it began to ping and vibrate wildly with a bunch of notifications.

"Your phone normally that busy?" I asked.

She shook her head. "Not this one. Where's my regular one, anyway?"

I pulled it from the nightstand drawer and handed it to her. She powered it on and set it down, then picked up the burner. I watched as her brow furrowed.

"There are sixteen missed texts and three missed calls." I watched the blood drain from her face as she read the messages. She looked up at me, fear coloring her features. "We missed one."

"What do you mean?" I asked, buttoning up and zipping my pants. *Mood: ruined.* She turned the phone around and showed me a text from a few hours ago.

V Boss: *Bitch, your boyfriend should learn to shoot better. I'm coming for you when you least expect it. You will finish the job for us, even if we have to tie you to a chair. Once you're done, I'm gonna shoot you in the head and dump your body in the ocean.*

She swallowed hard. "What should we do?"

I took the phone from her and read the other messages. They were similarly threatening in nature. "First off, this guy is really stupid. Threatening to kill you after you do the job for them?" I snorted. "Then who'd maintain the website? And why would you even finish it if you knew you were dead once the job was done?" I scrubbed a hand down my face. "I gotta show Viper."

She followed me downstairs, and I found Viper and MyAnna in the breakroom chatting. He held a coffee mug reading *Have a Nice Day,* but when he tipped it up to drink, there was a drawing of a hand giving the middle finger on the bottom.

"Boss, we have a problem." I opened the text and showed it to him.

He quickly read it and his brow furrowed. "Just fucking great."

"What's wrong?" Shadow asked, entering the breakroom.

He handed the phone to Craig, and he read it. "Fuck."

"The only thing we can do is let them come to us. I doubt they're still in the Virgin Islands. He must have had quite the mess to clean up," I said.

"Yep, ashes everywhere," Shadow said. "I'm sure he's pissed we killed all his cronies."

"You mean *you* killed them all," I said to him.

"We should have stayed and waited until they were all ash. Dumb oversight on my part," Viper said, setting his mug into the sink.

I clapped him on his good shoulder. "It's not your fault. When that last one didn't turn to ash, I assumed he was human. They were too far away for me to tell."

"So did I," Shadow said.

"No, the guy with the ponytail is the main kidnapper," Devon added. "I didn't even look back after he was shot. I should have noticed, as well."

I squeezed her to me. "It's okay, beautiful. It was pure chaos."

"Is Venom still here?" Viper asked.

"No," MyAnna said. "He and his little family left a couple minutes ago."

"Phoenix!" Viper called out.

He popped his head into the breakroom a few seconds later. "Yeah?"

Shadow showed him the text. He went to hand the phone to Shadow, but I took it.

"Not cool. I didn't realize we'd left one alive," Phoenix replied.

"We gotta think this through," Viper said. "The only way to end this is to draw him out. Can I see that please?" he asked me with his hand out.

I gave the phone to him.

"I say we reply to this. How about…" He began to type with his thumbs, and then raised his voice an octave, trying to sound female. "Don't threaten me, you asshole! You kidnapped me! I'm not working for you again."

Everyone laughed.

"Yes, that's exactly what I would have replied with," Devon said with a small chuckle.

"It's just gonna piss him off, but at least he'll know you got the messages," Viper said, hitting *send*.

The phone chimed a few seconds later. He read it aloud. "Yes, you will. You owe us for calling the feds." Viper chuckled and typed a reply as he recited it in the girl voice. "I don't owe you shit." He hit *send* and it chimed again immediately. He read the message and smiled. "Looks like this dick is changing his tune. He says, 'Fine, you cunt. Name your price but you will pay for what you did to my men.'" He looked at Devon. "What do you charge for something like this?"

She lifted a shoulder and let it fall. "I've only built simple websites and charge about a thousand for those. Tell him ten grand." She smirked. "Those fuckers are loaded."

He typed out a response and tapped *send*.

When a reply didn't come back right away, he handed the phone to Devon. "Let me know immediately if he responds."

"I will," she said. "But you do know I'm not doing that, right?"

"Of course you're not. We're just tricking him." I pulled her to me and kissed the top of her head. "Don't worry, nobody's going to harm you. This place is tightly guarded, and Bloome's working on a protection spell, too. I'm glad we got your stuff from the apartment since those assholes know where you live."

"Yeah, good call," Viper said.

The phone pinged in her hand. She read the text aloud: "Fine, you'll get the 10k once the job is complete. Start working on that shit now, bitch. You have one week, Rocky." She looked at us. "What should I do?"

I had an idea. "Tell them you're not starting without a two-thousand-dollar deposit. I might be able to trace this guy from the account. How were they paying you before?"

"Cash App," she said.

"Okay, tell him to use the same account for the deposit. I'll try to trace it."

She nodded and replied to the text.

"Good one," Shadow said.

The phone made a different noise. Devon looked down at it and grinned. "Deposit made."

"Let's go," I said, grabbing her hand. "You'll need to log into Cash App from the computer."

She rolled her eyes. "Duh, I know that."

"Then why haven't you ever tried to trace them when they were paying you before?" I asked.

Devon shrugged. "Because I didn't care who they were. They paid me consistently, and I didn't ask any questions."

"Fair enough."

25

PLAYGROUND CONFESSIONS

Devon

Six days later, my stress level was through the roof. I was getting multiple texts a day asking for updates on the site. I lied through my teeth, assuring him that I was working hard on it, all the while Parker was reassuring me that we'd be okay. We had to be patient. Spending every day wrapped up in his arms in the safety of his apartment helped to calm my anxiety and gave me hope that once this was over, we could try to have something together. Something normal and amazing.

The trace had been a dead end. They had their stuff protected pretty well, both the Cash App and the phone in general. It was also a prepaid cell with no name registered and we couldn't trace the location the texts were sent from.

"I'm getting cabin fever, handsome. Can we go out for a little bit?" I asked Parker as we sat in his office. We were almost done with the app program he'd started on a few weeks ago. I was helping him polish it up.

He looked over at me. "I don't know, we should probably stay inside until all of this is cleared up."

I bit my lip and batted my eyelashes at him. "Please? I just need some fresh air and a change of scenery. I'm feeling cooped up here."

"Okay. Let's finish this up. Then we'll go walk around the park."

Clapping, I squealed and kissed him on the cheek. "Yay."

God, I was turning into such a chocolate heart around him. What happened to the quiet, broody girl I was just a couple of weeks ago? Oh yeah, she was gone because she fell in love with the pretty boy with the big brain and an even bigger heart. He'd saved me from what was probably sure death, and he hadn't thought twice about it. I never thought I'd ever fall in love, but it was instantaneous when I met Parker. My soul knew his was its missing half.

We drove to the park, and after parking his bike in the lot, we walked hand-in-hand toward the play structures. I sat down on one of the swings and breathed in the fresh night air. A half-moon illuminated the park. It was quiet, just the two of us.

I squeaked when I felt my body propel forward. I craned my head back to see Parker pushing me on the swings.

"God, I haven't been on a swing since I was a child," I said. "Why don't I go to parks more often?"

He laughed and gave me another shove. "I don't know, why don't you? Oh yeah, because you're too busy on your computer, hacking into stuff."

I snorted. "Hey, you should talk. You're no better."

"Oh, but I am better," he said with a mischievous tone. He caught me by the waist on the upswing and held me there. After planting a kiss on the side of my neck, he let the swing go and I was propelled forward, my hair flailing in the wind with each swing.

As I swung, I felt so free. It was so nice to not be cooped up in my apartment, hoping for something better to come along. Being afraid to be in public for fear of people staring at me. Parker was helping me to open up and it was such a good feeling. I could literally feel my depression lifting. I no longer felt like I was stuck in my lonely, unhappy life forever.

On the next upswing, he held my waist again and let me go slowly to stop the propulsion. He went around and grabbed my hands, pulling me to a stand. He wrapped his arms around my waist and brushed some hair from my face. "I didn't think this was a good idea, but I'm glad you made me leave the clubhouse. I needed to get out, too. I didn't realize I had cabin fever as well. Thank you." He leaned down and kissed me.

I slung my arms around his neck and kissed him back. I couldn't explain with words what his touch did to me. The kisses alone caused my head to spin and butterflies to erupt in my stomach. When he made love to me, I felt like I was in another world. I had never experienced anything like it. There was no way I was ever going to let him go.

He broke the kiss and looked around before staring down into my eyes. "I love you."

I gazed deep into his eyes. "Why?"

Parker's brow furrowed. "What do you mean?"

Stroking my fingers along his cheek, I asked, "How can someone so perfect love someone so flawed like me?"

He frowned and pulled me closer to him with a sigh. "Devon, I've always been the type of guy who tried to find the little imperfections in the people I met. Then you came into my life, and I realized there were none to be found. You think you're flawed? You're not. You're perfectly imperfect. When are you going to see that? Nobody's perfect or flawless. Certainly not me. I've made my share of mistakes and sins and I'll be forever paying for them. I'll pay my penance to the universe by taking care of the other half of my soul—making sure she always knows she's loved. If you'd see yourself through my eyes, you'd know that you're the most beautiful woman in the world."

I looked down as tears I couldn't stop cascaded down my face in rivulets.

He put his finger under my chin and forced me to face him. He looked alarmed when he saw my tears and used both thumbs to wipe them away as he cradled my face. "Devon, love doesn't see imperfections. It's why they say it's blind. It can be a curse, but the blessing is why we were designed this way."

I gripped him tighter and buried my head into his chest. "Thank you for seeing through the scars and helping me find the real me.

She's been gone so long I never thought I'd get her back."

"Let's take a walk," he said, pointing to a small lake on the other side of the playground.

He gripped my hand and we walked in silence. I saw him occasionally look around to make sure we were safe. I knew he had a gun tucked into the back of his pants and a knife sheathed on his belt. He'd even given me a pistol to carry with me at all times, but of course I'd left it in his room at the clubhouse because I wasn't used to carrying it.

"What are we going to do once the deadline passes and I don't have a website for that jerk? Tomorrow's one week," I said as we strolled along the lakefront.

"The way I see it," Parker replied, "he's going to come looking for you when you ghost him—and you *will* be ghosting him. He's gonna go berserk. As soon as the sun goes down tomorrow night, we're going to head to your apartment. Viper and I will be inside, the other guys will be outside the building. Eagle's going to be in the van—our getaway driver."

"So, you discussed all of this already? Without me?" I felt hurt and left out.

He lifted my hand to his lips and placed a chaste kiss on my knuckles. "It's club business, beautiful. Usually the old ladies sit it out."

"But this directly involves me," I argued.

"If you really think about it, it doesn't. He'll never find you. You're safer in the clubhouse. Once he and whoever else decide to come after you, they're dead. Period."

I wasn't sure I liked that. I felt the need for some kind of vindication since they'd kidnapped and threatened me, but I supposed the fact that three of them were already dead... I should be content with that. "I don't know..."

"Look," Parker said, pointing to some geese and swans floating on the lake.

I stared at where he was pointing. "Beautiful creatures for sure."

"Don't feed them," he warned. "They turn into psychos. The geese, I mean."

Laughing, I said, "How do you know?"

"Lots of goose ponds in California. Do you know they'll actually hiss at you like a cat if you get too close to them?"

I bit back a smile. "No, I didn't, you little nature lover, you."

Parker leaned down and kissed me. "You're so cute."

"If you say so," I replied cheekily.

We kept walking around the lake, and he pulled his phone from his pocket. I watched him type out a text.

"Am I boring you?" I asked with a grin.

He chuckled and re-pocketed the phone. "Not at all. Told Viper I'd do half-hour watch-calls."

"What's that?" I asked.

"Oh, just a check-in to make sure we're okay. He wasn't happy when I told him we were going to the park. He doesn't think we should be in public."

"The way I see it, these psychos aren't going to try to kill me until they realize they're not getting their website. Am I right?"

He nodded. "Yes, but obviously, they're not above kidnapping. In fact, one more lap around the lake and we should go."

Sighing, I said, "Fine."

An hour later, we were back at the clubhouse.

"Where's Viper?" Parker asked Venom, who was sitting in the breakroom eating a bowl of cereal.

"Cobalt, in his office," he replied, looking up from his phone. He looked tired and had dark circles under his eyes.

"You all right, man?" Parker asked.

He nodded. "Yeah, fine. It's easier if I stay here at night and then go back to the house to sleep in the morning. Kalissa's up with the baby on and off, and since she's the only one who can feed him, it's best if I just let her do her thing."

"Ah, okay," Parker said, dragging me by the hand toward the walkway.

We found Viper in his office, and he looked stressed. Parker knocked on the doorframe. "Boss?"

He looked up at us and told us to come in.

"Just checking in. Everything set for tomorrow night?" Parker asked.

"Yes." Viper looked at me. "Any more texts or calls?"

"He texts me a couple times a day to check in, seeing how the website's going." I swallowed hard.

"What do you tell him?" Viper asked.

"Mainly bullshit, that I'm working hard on it and that I can't guarantee it'll be done by the promised date but that I'll let him know when it's finished."

"Good, that will keep him hanging on."

"He still insists it has to be done by tomorrow. He's a bit of a dick, honestly."

Viper chuckled. "Yeah? Well, so am I. He's gonna be sorry if he shows at your place."

"So I've been told." I squeezed Parker's hand tighter.

"We'll be in my apartment if you need us. Just text," my handsome vampire told his boss.

He looked at us with an expression I couldn't decipher, and then said, "Will do."

We went up the stairs and locked ourselves in Parker's apartment.

"I need a shower," I said.

"Me too," he replied.

After Parker started the shower, we stripped our clothes off and stepped inside. I plunged my head under the hot, pounding water and groaned at how good it felt. When I opened my eyes, he was standing in front of me, gazing at my body before he lazily looked into my eyes. He grabbed the loofah, put some soap on it from an auto-dispenser attached to the wall, and leaned down. Starting at my ankles, he slowly scrubbed every inch of my legs. When he reached the apex between my thighs, he spread me apart and ran his finger over my clit, then washed me there before moving up the flat of my stomach and onto my breasts. Sliding the loofah across my chest and over my shoulders, he then moved to my arms. Once they were soapy, he kissed me hard before turning me around and working on my back, waist, hips, and then ass. Once my legs were soaped up, I was walked backward, with him staring into my eyes, and rinsed off. He turned me around and rinsed my front while his erection pressed into my tailbone. I heard the shampoo dispenser right before he began massaging my hair with suds. After I rinsed off my hair, I squeezed some shampoo into my hand and lifted my arms to massage it onto his head. The loofah was still soapy, so with slow movements, I washed every inch of his body. Once we were suds-free, Parker reached down to spread my lips apart before massaging my extremely swollen clit with his fingers. I could barely get the conditioner out of the bottle and into my hair before my legs began to shake. I dropped the bottle and it rolled to the other side of the massive shower. My climax was building so fast with what he was doing with his fingers, I thought I was going to slip and fall. When he sealed his hot mouth around my nipple, I exploded, mumbling his name like a curse while I grappled the walls of the shower for something to hold onto.

Parker picked me up under each leg, my head falling back under the water as it cascaded over my hair. I whimpered when his dick thrust into me. I gripped his shoulders for leverage and gazed into his eyes as he fucked me hard and fast, my legs wrapped around his waist. The friction from his thick cock was causing a tidal wave of lust to begin to swirl in my womb. I looked at the vein throbbing slowly on his neck, leaned down, and sank a fang into it.

We both groaned while I sucked hard, his blood flowing down my throat while I rolled my hips in time with his. He picked up speed, grunting as the friction from his thrusts made me shudder when another orgasm tore through my body. I squeezed his cock with my slick walls right as he stilled, shooting his load into me with an growl.

"Fuck…" he breathed.

We stood there like that, breathless and seeing stars, my head dipped into the crease where his shoulder met his neck. Once we caught our breath, he slowly put me down, turned off the now cool water, and helped me out of the shower. After drying off, we fell asleep, exhausted and happy.

EAT ME

Face

The barrage of texts got so bad, I had to take the phone from Devon and power it down so we could get some sleep. The part of the operation where we planned to ignore him had now gone into effect. Once this guy became furious at being ghosted, he'd show up at her apartment and try to nab her again. We'd already determined he was predictable like that.

I blinked my eyes open, after one of the best sleeps I'd had in a long time, and immediately reached over to the side of the bed, just wanting to pull Devon into my arms. I was greeted with nothing but cold sheets. I sat up, alarmed. My eyes scanned the room until I found her curled up on the plush chair in the corner of the room. She wore my T-shirt and was looking at something on her phone.

Immediately relieved, I said, "Good morning, beautiful."

She looked up at me. "Hi."

"I hate that I need more sleep than you," I replied around a yawn.

Devon shrugged. "You'll need less as time goes on. I'm much older than you, remember? In fact, you really shouldn't be dating cougars. They bite."

I threw back the covers with a chuckle and stood. "Come here."

She set the phone down and walked over to me. Her sexy bed hair and the way her T-shirt fell right to the top of her creamy thighs made her look good enough to eat. I wrapped her in a hug.

"I love waking up with you here."

"Same," she replied.

"I'm so glad this is going to be over tonight," she murmured. "I'm so used to my boring life that this has been so stressful. My anxiety's through the roof."

"We'll be in and out, it'll be a piece of cake," I said into her hair before kissing the top of her head and squeezing her reassuringly.

"I'm coming with," she said.

I released her and looked down at her, gently gripping both her biceps. "No, you're not."

The stubborn set of her lips and the look in her eyes I'd already come to learn colored her features. "Yes, I am. I'm not gonna sit here and chew off all my fingernails while I wait for you to get back. All of this crap is because of me. My bad decisions to work for criminals and not care about anything but money. I want to help."

"No," I said. "It's safer for you here."

"I can take care of myself, and I want in on the revenge."

I gritted my teeth. "Then you'll wait in the van."

Devon lifted her chin. "The hell I will." She wandered into the bathroom and closed the door.

Shaking my head, I went into my closet and pulled out the tactical clothing and boots. *She* will *wait in the van.*

I powered up the burner phone and read the twelve text messages. There were two voicemails, each threatening her using voice-altering technology. I saved them and then set the phone down.

Devon came out of the bathroom smelling like toothpaste and still looking angry. I reached down, tore the T-shirt off over her head, and gripped her upper arms. "Get your ass into the shower. Now. Or no Dick for you." I looked down at my raging hard-on. We just called him *Dick* now. *So original.*

With wide green eyes, she nodded and turned around, obeying like a good little girl. I could only hope she'd be that compliant later when she wasn't threatened with not getting any D.

"She may be the stubbornest of all the old ladies," Viper said, shaking his head.

"You're telling me," I muttered. "I can't believe she agreed to wait in the van."

Viper and I stood in Devon's living room, armed to the teeth and dressed in our tactical gear. We'd been here three hours. Shadow and Venom were outside the building hiding in the shadows. Phoenix had a pre-arranged vacation planned with Jemini. He'd wanted to cancel it to help us out, but we told him it wasn't necessary. This should be an easy enough job.

"I told Andy to text us if she leaves or tries to leave." Viper walked over to the computer and shook the mouse.

I already had my hand covering my face because I knew what he was going to see. He laughed. "Someone's a fangirl."

"Trust me, I asked her to change it. She won't." I walked over to the workstation. "Do you need to look something up?"

"Nah, was just bored. Wanted to see what kind of stuff she had on here. So far, I can see she likes guys with six-packs and long walks on the beach." He pointed to the monitor above it depicting a Hawaiian shoreline.

"Something like that," I said, trying not to smile.

A noise from the back of the apartment caught out attention. Viper put his finger to his lips and raised his face covering. I raised mine and followed him. With our backs flat against the hallway wall right outside Devon's bedroom, we could hear the window opening. I peeked quickly around the doorframe and saw a man jump inside from the fire escape and land on Devon's bed. With his gloved fingers, Viper counted down from three. When he reached one, we stormed into the room. The man, who was just about to look in Devon's closet with his gun drawn, was taken by surprise when I kicked the pistol out of his hand and it went clattering to the ground. He grunted in pain and then tried to scurry past us. Viper tackled him to the ground.

I pushed the com on my earpiece. "We've got one inside the bedroom."

"He's human," Viper said, holding him down with his forearm across his neck.

"Human," I added into the mic.

"We've got two sitting in a van on a side street. They're wearing some kind of white masks," Shadow said. "Devon says those are the masks they wear."

"Apprehend them and bring them up here," I said into the earpiece.

Viper stood and said, "On your belly, now. Hands behind your head."

The man complied.

Viper activated his earpiece. "Bring Devon up with you."

"Roger that," Venom replied.

A few seconds later, we heard a gunshot. Within seconds, the front door opened, and we went into the living room, Viper grappled with the human before tossing him into a chair. Shadow and Venom walked in with two men in handcuffs Bloome had spelled so they were unbreakable. They wore clownish white theatrical masks, one with a frown, one with a smile. One had a long blond ponytail tied at the back of his head.

They were plunked down on the sofa, then Shadow kicked one in the knee so hard, the guy cried out and started whimpering. "Fuck!"

"This one shot me," Shadow snapped, pointing to his bicep.

I looked at it. "Grazed you, but still."

Devon came over to me and put her arm around my waist.

"These them?" I asked.

She nodded. "I'm pretty sure. At least one of them. They all wore those masks."

"Where's our fucking website, Frank?" Ponytail asked.

I stalked over to him, ripped his mask off, and punched him in the face. "Shut the fuck up with that shit." Then, I tore the other's mask off and tossed it to the coffee table.

Ponytail slid his jaw back and forth and grinned up at me. "How chivalrous." He looked at Devon. "Enjoy it while it lasts, Frank, because you're dead." He had amusement dancing in his brown eyes. "All of you. Especially you, you smelly-ass wolf."

Venom chuckled with his arm folded. "You don't look like you're in the position to be making threats."

"Who are you fuckers, anyway? Sending a human in here to do your dirty work?" Viper asked, pointing to the man in the chair glaring daggers at us.

Ponytail replied, "He was just casin' the joint, weren't you, Len?"

Len narrowed his eyes at the vampires. "You could have warned me there was more than one vamp in here, Gene. I was only supposed to snatch the girl."

I lifted an eyebrow. "You sent a human in here to kidnap a vampire? You are as stupid as you look."

Len pointed to his pocket. "I have a tranq in my pocket, was gonna drug her, then toss her out the window to the guys."

"We're three stories up!" Devon cried, throwing her arms up.

"You'd heal, they told me," Len replied, now looking frightened.

"Shut up, Len," the other said through gritted teeth. His black-colored eyes were glossy, probably from when he'd been kicked.

"No, Dean. You guys promised to turn me, but you keep putting it off. One more job, one more job. Blah, blah. Well, I'm done." He looked at us. "I'll tell you anything you want to know." He glanced at his vampire cronies. "And you both can fuckin' eat me."

"You probably shouldn't say that in a roomful of vamps," Devon said with a sardonic laugh.

"Call the BSI," Viper said to me.

"You got it," I replied, pulling out my phone. We'd decided earlier not to kill them, but turn them in instead—help the FBI with the website case.

Gene laughed. "You guys are a bunch of pussies. Calling the cops? You think they can keep us in prison?"

I listened as Viper explained that their special prison was made to hold supernatural creatures as Nolan Bishop's line trilled in my ear.

"Agent Bishop," he answered quietly after four rings.

"We've apprehended the suspects from the human trafficking site. Two vamps, one human."

He perked up and I could hear a lamp clicking on. "Is that so?"

"Yes, come get them before I kill them," I replied, staring at the two vampires.

"Clubhouse?" he asked.

"No," I replied and stated Devon's address and apartment number.

"It'll take me a while to get everyone assembled. Be there in thirty to forty minutes."

"Better hurry." I ended the call.

Dean looked over at Len. "We're gonna kill you if we get sent to jail. You hear me, you snitch?"

Shadow punched him in the jaw. "Shut it."

I had an idea. "Give me the tranq," I said to Len, holding my hand out.

He cautiously removed it from his coat pocket and handed it to me. I pulled the cap off with my teeth and spit it out on the ground. I looked at the vampires in the room. "Hold Ponytail down."

Gene protested and tried to kick out while Viper and Shadow held him down. Devon and Venom made sure Dean didn't try to get up.

I shot exactly half of the tranquilizer into Gene's neck before shooting the other half into Dean's.

"It won't knock them completely out, but they'll be a lot more compliant when the feds get here," I said.

"Dean and Gene. How cute," Devon said. "Those your real names?"

Gene attempted to flip her off but began to drift in and out of consciousness.

"You're my hero," Devon said, putting her arms around my waist and staring up at me as we waited for the agents.

"I just want this all behind us," I said. "Evil is evil, they had to be stopped."

"I agree," she said, pressing her cheek against my chest.

"Do you think they're going to send me to prison?" Len asked as the other two dozed.

"If you cooperate, I'm sure they'll work with you," Viper said. "Breaking and Entering and Attempted Kidnapping are serious charges, so I suggest you tell the feds they forced you, threatened your family, whatever else you can think of."

"Also, don't become a vampire. It's not glamorous. Stay human, you'll thank me later," I said to him, stroking Devon's back.

Len looked down. "I've been bullied my whole life. I just wanted to stop being so afraid all the time. To be a badass, get some revenge. Ya know?"

"Take some martial arts classes. Learn how to shoot a perfect grouping. Hit the gym. You'll be amazed how empowered you'll feel," Venom said.

"Cops are here," Andy said into our earpieces after a few silent minutes passed.

A knock on the door caught our attention. Shadow looked through the peephole with his gun up and then holstered it before opening the door.

Agents Bishop and Shields, dressed in tactical gear, along with two other men wearing the same, came inside. "These them?" Bishop asked.

"Vamps." I pointed to the two sleeping beauties. "Gene and Dean." I pointed to Len. "Human, very willing to cooperate."

Shields instructed him to stand where she handcuffed him. She looked at Bishop. "I'll take him alone and meet you at headquarters."

He nodded and we watched her take Len out. We all lowered our face coverings now that the Len was gone.

"What did you give them?" Bishop asked.

"Len was kind enough to bring a tranquilizer with him. We only had one so they each got half. It won't last long, so you should hurry," Viper said.

The two men, who I could tell were vampires, threw the thugs over their shoulders in a fireman's carry and left.

"Thank you," Bishop said, shaking our hands. He looked at Devon. "Are you all right?"

"Yes, I'm all good. Thank you, Agent."

"I suggest you stay off the Dark Web, young lady." He grinned knowingly.

"Hey. I'm older than you," she said, lifting her chin.

He winked a green eye at her. "I know."

Bishop headed toward the door.

"Keep us updated on the case, huh?" I asked.

"Absolutely." He opened the door then stopped with his hand on the edge. "Thanks for not killing them. We're going to make an example out of them. They'll make for great training videos."

"You got vamps working for you, huh?" Shadow asked, jutting his chin toward the window.

"Everyone's got a price," he replied with a nod and then left.

"Kovah's wife's a vamp, and she works for them," Venom added.

"That's true." I looked at my love. "Do you need anything else from here before we head back to the clubhouse?"

She chewed her lip and looked at her workstation. "That stuff cost a lot of money. Can I bring it?"

Viper chuckled. "There's a spare office next to Face's."

"Jemini was gonna take it," I replied.

"We can share," Devon said. "I like her."

"She likes you, too." I kissed her nose.

"Let me grab some more clothes and toiletries, then we can go."

"No hoodies," I said as she made her way toward her room.

She disappeared into the bedroom, and the guys looked at me. "What?" I asked.

"Just never thought I'd see you smitten," Shadow said with a chuckle as he pursed his lips and batted his eyelashes.

"Eat me," I said, biting back a grin and heading to the bedroom to help Devon.

EPILOGUE

LOVE EXISTS

Devon

Three Months Later

I stared in awe at my reflection. "I can't believe it," I breathed.

"It's not cheap, but it's the best on the market," Jemini said, holding up the small bottle. "A lot of full-coverage makeup doesn't really cover as much as they say. The best way to test them is on a tattoo." She had her skirt pulled down below her hipbone where a tattoo of a flower sat. She took three different foundations and used a small sponge to dab on each area of the tat. The one she'd just used on my face hid the part of the flower completely. You could still see part of the flower under the other two samples.

"That's a really cool trick. I don't have any tattoos though."

She grinned as she wiped the makeup off her hip with a wet cloth. "Face does."

I pursed my lips to keep from smiling. "You tried this on Phoenix, didn't you?"

She nodded. "Yes, but don't tell anyone or he'll kill me. His coloring is closer to yours and his tat is much bigger so it worked better."

I laughed.

"I got each of my bridesmaids a special gift, so it had to be perfect. This is my gift to you for being in my wedding." She kissed my cheek.

My eyes welled up. "Thank you."

Jemini put her hand on my shoulder as she sat in the chair next to mine in front of the vanity inside my and Parker's apartment. "Listen, I think you're beautiful without any makeup. You're lucky you don't need it like me."

I rolled my eyes at her.

"But I also know how self-conscious you are about your scarring." She tapped my cheek with her index finger. "I wanted to give you this so if you go out in public, you don't feel like you have to hide under those hoods. You may feel a sense of normalcy while wearing it. Help your anxiety and all that."

"You don't know how much this means to me. I've tried makeup before, but it just looked caked on, and I felt stupid wearing it. I've never had a female friend before to help me like this. It means the world to me." I hugged her and she hugged me back, her ring getting caught in my hair.

"Whoops," she said, picking the hair out of it. "It's too damn big."

I smiled. "Hell no, it's not. It's beautiful." I stared at the two-carat diamond set in platinum. Phoenix had taken her to Miami for a few nights and had proposed on the beach under the moon. Us girls had all gathered around like hens after they'd returned to hear the story, squealing.

I shooed her. "Now, we're gonna be late for your final fitting, so go get your stuff and I'll meet you downstairs."

"You're right." She looked at her watch. "See you in a bit."

She left the apartment and I stared into the mirror again. I turned my face from left to right. The scars were still there but barely visible. I put a little contour, blush, and highlighter on, then brushed some mascara on my lashes and some pink gloss on my lips. I had my hair in a high ponytail and wore my favorite ripped jeans and a lime-green long-sleeved shirt.

I slid my feet into my new Chucks and grabbed my wallet, keys, and phone.

Parker came out of the bathroom, the steam following him out. He wore nothing but a towel, his hair wet and flopped into his face. He took my breath away.

"God, I want to lick you right now," I said, wetting my lips and tasting the strawberry flavor.

He looked up from adjusting his towel and went to speak but froze. "I… Oh, my God… Devon. You look. I mean, wow!"

I grinned. "Thanks. Jemini's a miracle worker."

He stepped closer to me, and the warm steam felt good. "You know I think you're beautiful without all this stuff on your face, as well, right? My question is, how does it make you feel?"

"I know you do, and that's why I love you." I put my hand on his perfectly smooth skin and sharp jaw. "The makeup was a gift from her. She seems to be some kind of mind-reader or something. She could tell how self-conscious I was in public." I blew out a breath. "Honestly, I really like the makeup. It won't be worn all the time, but it'll help me not be so anxious."

"If you love it, then then I love it," he replied. "And while I agree Jemini's got wicked intuition, it doesn't take spidey senses to tell that you wanted to hide from the world. I hope you don't feel like you have to now." He kissed my nose and went to walk around me toward his dresser. I grabbed his towel off his waist and whipped him in his cute little butt with it.

"Hey!" he said, starting toward me, but I ran out the door and down the stairs giggling.

As Jemini, Bloome, MyAnna, Kalissa, and I piled into Kalissa's new minivan, we made small talk about the wedding coming up on Saturday. As they chatted excitedly, I stared down at baby Jameson, who was blinking wide blue eyes up at me. I smiled at him, and he beamed a big, toothless grin back at me. It was hard to believe he was going to turn into a big, ferocious wolf when he was grown. I let him grip my pinky finger with his little hand, and I looked out at the early evening sky. I couldn't believe how much my life had changed in six months. I went from an anxiety-ridden, shy, hermit girl who never left her home, to a woman with friends and a gorgeous man who loved me. Actual friends who didn't try to use me for anything or treat me any differently. Sharing an office with Jemini and helping them with all the tech stuff at the club had been really rewarding. I felt like I was living in a fantasy or dream I hoped I'd never wake from.

"You look good enough to eat," Parker leaned down and whispered in my ear.

"Later." I winked up at him. He looked absolutely breathtaking in a black tuxedo. All the guys did.

The Cobalt Room was packed with people. Gabriel and Jemini had had a huge wedding at a nearby cathedral where her parents paid for the grand affair. Her mother hadn't been too happy that she wanted the reception here, but she ensured her parents the place was rented out and it would be private. I looked over to see Jemini and Jermaine holding hands, facing each other, and not speaking. She'd tried to explain the twin telepathy to me, but it was hard to wrap my brain around being able to read someone else's mind.

I looked down at my long dark-blue dress with the plunging neckline and slit. We'd all worn silk scarves tied to the side around our necks as part of the ensemble, and something told me Jemini had chosen that accessory for me—because of my scars. None of the other girls seemed to mind it, and I thought it looked like a nice addition to the dress.

Viper went onstage and stood in front of the band. He held a champagne flute up, tapping a spoon against it. "Toast. Everyone, grab a drink."

Parker and I already held club sodas.

Viper lifted his glass, MyAnna by his side. "To Gabriel and Jemini. Wishing you a lifetime of love and happiness.

Congratulations on the most important union of your life. May you two always find love and hope in the company of one another."

"Here, here!" everyone said.

Parker clinked his glass with mine. "Cheers." We took a sip and then kissed.

A man in a suit with brown eyes and a beautiful woman on his arm approached us. He gave Parker a back-pounding man-hug. "What's up, pretty boy?"

"Kovah, Manta, this is my girlfriend, Devon."

"Nice to meet you," Manta said, dipping her head.

Kovah nodded at me as he shoved a cracker and some olives into his mouth. "Hey."

"You as well." I smiled at them.

"Glad to see you ditched the douchebag glasses," Parker said, chuckling.

I smacked Parker's chest with the back of my hand. "Parker!"

Kovah laughed. "Nah, he's right. I put these stupid contacts in when I have to do fancy shit or work events with the missus here." He pulled down one brown contact lens to reveal a strange iris, it was whitish-blue with just a small black pupil.

"I see," I said, wondering what happened to his eyes and making a mental note to ask Parker later. He didn't seem to be blind. He was also eating food and smelled like a vamp, so I was confused.

"How's New York?" Parker asked.

He shrugged and grabbed a piece of cheese, popping it into his mouth. "It's all right. Gotta wait ten years before we can come back here."

"It'll go by fast," Manta said, squeezing his hand.

"She's right," I added.

"Sorry, this is a private event."

We turned to see Dash holding his hand up to an older gentleman in a prim suit. He looked familiar, as did the beautiful brunette on his arm.

"Isn't that—"

My eyes widened. "Gregory."

"Excuse us," Parker said to Kovah and Manta.

I rushed over to Dash. "It's okay, he's a friend."

"Yes, I'm terribly sorry to crash your party," Gregory said to Dash.

I nodded at Dash. "We're good."

Gregory looked at me. "Rocky! You look so different! I hardly recognized you!"

I winked. "I clean up all right."

He patted my hand. "You weren't answering your cell, dear, and I wasn't sure if you had made it out of your, ah, predicament earlier, so I came here to see Mr. Face." He shook Parker's hand.

"It's just Face. Or Parker, if you'd like," he said, chuckling.

"Well, I won't take much of your time, I wanted to check on you and introduce you to my wife. Sue Ann, this is Rocky and Parker. Rocky helped me find you."

"My name is actually Devon," I said with a grin.

"Ooh, all these secret spy names. How exciting," Sue Ann drawled with a giggle. "Nice to meet you both. Thank you for helping my Gregory find me. I thought I was destined to a long life of solitude."

I glanced around and lowered my voice. "Why did you become a vampire, if you don't mind me asking?"

She glanced at her husband. "I knew he was a vampire right before he left me and the children. I was a witch, well, I still am. I'm now both. I was trying to figure out a way to let him know that I knew, but then he was just gone one night. I started to give up looking for him after a few years, but I had to leave my options open. I requested to be turned by a local vampire so I could have more time to find him."

"I say you made the right choice," Parker said.

"I, of course, think she should have just lived a long, happy life and hope we met in the next, but I can't say I'm disappointed." Gregory lifted her hand to his lips and kissed her knuckles.

"We'll be out of your hair now," she said and placed a cool hand on my bare forearm. "Thank you again, Devon. If you ever need anything, please don't hesitate to ask."

"Sue Ann closed her bakery in Minneapolis. We're opening an all-night diner on the outskirts here. There will be pies galore."

"We'll send all our human friends your way," I replied.

They each hugged me and left.

We watched as Gabriel and Jemini entered the dancefloor, her long white gown dragging behind her. Bloome quickly bustled up the train and pinned it to the back before two began to dance, where a band played a cover of "Love Exists" by Amy Lee. I watched as Jemini stared up into Gabriel's eyes and the way he gazed at her as if she was the only woman on earth.

Parker stroked my bare shoulder with his fingers while his arm was draped around me. I looked around the Cobalt Room and couldn't imagine a place filled with more love than this one at this very moment.

Jemini and Jermaine's parents danced on the dance floor, staring at each other like newlyweds. I'd been told her mother recently got a second chance at life.

Harlan and Kalissa were dancing in place, Venom holding the baby on his shoulder as he held his wife's hand and stared down at her.

Craig and Bloome stood facing each other, holding a drink in one hand, their other hands linked before Shadow reached up and stroked her cheek, then bent down and kissed her.

Vane and MyAnna danced in place, Viper's hand on the small

of her back as he whispered something in her ear that made her giggle.

Eagle and his human girlfriend Amber sat at a table holding hands, Andy's fingers playing with the enormous diamond ring on her left hand.

Kovah grabbed Manta's hand and led her to the dance floor, where he stared down into her eyes, saying something to her that caused a big smile to break out on her pretty face before she threw her head back and laughed.

I smiled when Fox and Ally joined everyone on the dance floor and then kissed as he pulled her close. Took them long enough to admit they wanted to be together.

Grabbing Parker's drink, I set it down along with mine and led him to the dance floor, where we congratulated the new bride and groom again and then danced as Parker held me tight.

"Hey, I have a question," he said.

"What's that?" I asked, gazing up at him.

"Why did you change the background of my monitors to a beach, a space constellation, Paris at night, and a field of flowers?"

I lifted a shoulder. "I wanted to give you something pretty to look at."

His face went serious, his hands leaving my waist to gently grip my face as he stared into my eyes. "I already have that, Devon. From the time I wake up each evening to the time I fall asleep in the morning."

I bit my lip as tears stung my eyes. His arms found my waist again, and we swung slowly together, my cheek against his chest. As the singer crooned about love making no sense and having no name, and how it can bring you to tears and then set your heart on fire, I knew there were no truer words. Love was the ultimate contradictory emotion, and it had taken me through all of them. It could shatter your heart and was the only thing that could mend it. It was a painful lesson and the most rewarding one.

I looked up at Parker. "I love you, handsome."

He bent down to deliver me a sensual, head-spinning kiss and then whispered, "I love you more, beautiful."

THE END

AUTHOR'S NOTE:

If you've reached the end of this series, congratulations! This series was a long time coming, and from the time Kovah discovered them in his book a few years ago when that dude would not stop chattering in my ear, I knew the Nighthawks would need their own series. If the back and forth between past and present took you out of the story, I apologize. These guys just had so much story to tell, and I had to get it down as they spoke to me. I wanted y'all to see what they'd been through to bring them to where and who they are now. How they became the men, the vampires, who persevered and were rewarded with eternal love. If you loved the series, I would be so humbled if you could hop on whatever retailer and/or Goodreads and leave a review. Indie authors like me rely on reviews from readers like you! Thank you again for reading about my Nighthawks. This was my first MC series and I loved it so much, I have a feeling I'll be doing more in the future.
Love you guys. ~C.J.

SERIES ACKNOWLEDGMENTS:

Thank you, Amabel, for finding all my stupid typos and dumb missing words!
Thank you, Heather, for finding the rest of my silly mistakes, and for being my alpha!
Thank you to my son Austin for all the help with computer accuracy. You know your mama's not that smart!
Thank you, Kellie for my beautiful book covers and graphics. You're the GOAT!
Thank to my faithful beta and ARC readers. You guys are the bomb dot com!

NIGHTHAWKS MC SERIES

Viper

Shadow

Phoenix

Venom

Face

ABOUT THE AUTHOR

C.J. is a USA Today bestselling author living in Colorado but wishes she was someplace warmer. She loves the SF 49ers and has a weakness for expensive shoes. She's the author of over 40 novels and short stories that contain both fantasy and paranormal romance with kickass heroines and strong alphas. Having recently retired from a twenty-year career in federal law enforcement, she's looking forward to the next chapter in life.

She can be found on Facebook, Instagram, and on her website, cjpinard.com.

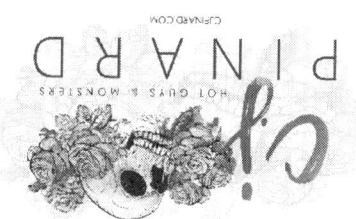

PINARD HOUSE
PUBLISHING

Use your device's QR code reader to get a link to all of C.J.'s books!

Made in the USA
Columbia, SC
16 September 2022